by the same author

A PERFECT MATCH

The man who had everything lies at the bottom of the quarry, having received the wages of sin.

Above him a group of people gather in the gloom near his abandoned Mercedes. They are all people whose lives he has touched, but only one of them knows they are all free from his blackmailing and bullying now.

Or are they? It seems that from the grave Alan Blake's influence is still real enough. Real enough to frighten Frankie, who was never afraid of him in life – real enough to set at each other's throats people who love each other. And it is skinny red-headed fighting Frankie, at odds with the world, who takes it all on her insubstantial shoulders, determined that Alan will hurt no-one else.

But the eighth deadly sin, that of omission, is one shared by each of the people in the little frightened group at the edge of the pit.

In this, Jill McGown's second suspense novel, she shows again her talent for creating real people for us to care about, in an intriguing mixture of intricate plot and intricate relationships, a glimpse into the reality of life and death in 'the smiling and beautiful countryside'. It is an exciting successor to *A Perfect Match*.

JILL McGOWN
RECORD OF SIN

M
MACMILLAN

First published 1985 by
MACMILLAN LONDON LIMITED
4 Little Essex Street London WC2R 3LF
and Basingstoke

Associated companies in Auckland, Delhi, Dublin, Gaborone, Hamburg, Harare, Hong Kong, Johannesburg, Kuala Lumpur, Lagos, Manzini, Melbourne, Mexico City, Nairobi, New York, Singapore and Tokyo.

McGown, Jill
    Record of Sin.
    I. Title
    823'.914[F] PR6063.A219/
    ISBN 0-333-38799-6

Typeset by Bookworm
Printed and bound by
Anchor Brendon Ltd, Tiptree, Essex

With grateful thanks to June, Tom and Vernon
and all the staff of Corby ITEC
for the generous use of their facilities and their time.

It is my belief, Watson, founded upon my experience, that the lowest and vilest alleys of London do not present a more dreadful record of sin than does the smiling and beautiful countryside.

Copper Beeches
Arthur Conan Doyle

Prologue

Twelve-thirty on a Saturday afternoon in July, and the villages known as the Caswells (pronounced *Cazzells* by the locals) were receiving their weekend wash and brush-up.

In Lower Caswell, the soft summer air was filled with the drones and hums of hover-mowers and electric hedge-trimmers, the whines of power drills and the revving of car engines being tuned to the perfection only the amateur demands. Hoses gushed water on to gleaming hatchback saloons and occasionally on to small children in bathing trunks, to their squealing delight. From somewhere, a transistor radio swelled the summer chorus and a tennis ball hit the grazed knee of a diminutive batsman to an impassioned cry of 'How's *that?*' from the bowler. The batsman accepted defeat graciously; it would be his turn to bowl and he fancied that the tarmac driveway would take a bit of spin.

This was the new development, the middle-range housing built to accommodate the needs of the young executive and his family. The walks and avenues were contained within the estate boundary roads and the dark red brick, fashioned into the would-be elegance of days gone by, was surrounded by cobbled courtyards with mock-Victorian lamp standards and fronted by Georgian garage doors.

In the small garden of one house a man in his mid-thirties, wearing a white sweatshirt and denim shorts, waged war on the long grass around his flowering cherry with a machine that sounded like a distressed wasp. His wife knelt by the path, trying to decide which were weeds and which were plants, but her heart was not in her task. He was tall, well built and dark, with a thin, impassive face – she was fairer, with a tendency to plumpness. The Rainfords had just had their Saturday morning row, so no

9

pleasantries passed between them.

The chevrons at the side of the road warned of the sharp, steep bend to the left, after which came the pub that served the Caswells. The Duke's Head was doing good business, the car park was full, and the grass verge was chock-a-block with the cars of the visitors – the people who came in from Market Brampton to sample the delights of the countryside. The garden at the rear was overflowing with lager-drinking, laughing groups who packed the wooden tables and spilled over on to the grass. There followed the rows of terraced houses which had once housed the quarry workers and, across from them, the surviving shops. A grocer's and a general store which was seeking sub-post office status in view of the new development were all that was left. The other shops had long since been converted into desirable residences, except for one casualty of the by-pass, a tea shop, up for sale with no takers.

The by-pass was just visible from there, as the sun glinted on the chromium and glass of the cars that no longer roared through the villages, and this was the point at which Long Caswell officially began. On either side of the road, on rising, wooded land, the village was strung out haphazardly like a broken string of pearls. The ground sloped gently at first, then dramatically, as it climbed out of the valley. The large gardens were well stocked and well kept and the long gravel driveways led to converted stables, to kitchen gardens and summerhouses. These houses had back stairs leading to servants' quarters, few of which were put to their original use. The odd one, however, could boast a live-in mother's help with own TV.

Saturday in Long Caswell was more traditional; the real enthusiasts and the part-time gardeners had never quite come to terms with electric gardening and the soothing click of hand-shears could be heard to a background of motor mowers chugging their way up and down the striped lawns. Exhaust fumes mingled with the cut grass and this smell of summer was carried on the air through the open windows of the master bedroom of one house. Inside, a couple were dressing after a late, leisurely breakfast. Richard Hascombe was a strongly built and fit fifty-two, with greying dark hair, close-cropped to prevent it curling too riotously. His companion was just under half his age and looked even younger than that.

Across the road, and a few hundred yards up the hill, was the last house in the village. A woman in her early forties sat at the table in the pine-clad kitchen, preferring its shaded coolness to the climbing sun. The only sound in the house was the quiet whirr of the extractor fan, and she thought she was alone. Her dark, casually well-cut hair was unbrushed, her face devoid of make-up. She looked tired; she had poured a cup of tea but it was cold now. Her husband was out or she would not be looking the way she did. She started as the door opened suddenly, but it was only her son. He was sixteen, brown-eyed, and very like her. He was taller than his stepfather now, his long legs encased in the inevitable blue denim. He said hello and took the kitchen stairs two at a time, up to his studio.

The road ran on for almost three miles through what was technically Upper Caswell but which consisted only of bright yellow fields of oilseed rape, skirted by the woodland which swept round behind the fields to meet the old quarry road. It was closed now, but you could still see where it had branched off the main Caswells road to run round the old workings, long abandoned. Nature had partially grassed over the scar and the savage bite out of the hillside lent a touch of drama to the unexciting landscape. The steep, dangerous side of the quarry was at the far end where the old road almost vanished as it met the wood. The sheer drop had once been fenced off but the fence had gone after years of wind and weather. The calls to have it replaced had grown less and less urgent as people simply got used to it.

The quietness of Upper Caswell was barely disturbed by the discreet rumble of a 747, just shimmeringly visible in the blue sky, ahead of its streaming vapour trails. A second later, the peace was shattered by the angry snarl of an airforce jet, scything its way through the air as it skimmed the valley.

The Caswells road curved again, just beyond the quarry turn-off, and ran on to where it met the by-pass in a complexity of painted arrows and diagonal stripes, traffic signs and directions. It was here on weekdays that the Caswells commuters had to wait forever to make the right turn to Market Brampton. Lorries

11

rattled their way into the old town, shaking the houses and knocking chips off the ones that stood too close to the road. They rumbled past the end-of-terrace house where a telephone rang and was automatically answered. A girl's voice apologised to the caller for her absence; the caller left a message. A newspaper boy wedged a paper in the letter box and remounted his bicycle, bumping off the pavement and pedalling across the side street to his next port of call.

And the keys to the skeleton-cupboards began turning in the locks.

Chapter One

1

Joyce Rainford heard the phone, but she didn't dare answer it. 'It'll be for you,' she said. 'Telephone.'

'What?' said Mark, switching off the lawnmower.

'It'll be for you,' Joyce repeated, telegraphic communication having replaced the earlier silence. Joyce felt guilty, because she had in a way engineered the apparently routine row so that they would end up not speaking. That way, she wouldn't have to say what was really on her mind, what had been on her mind for weeks.

Mark deliberately brushed past her on his way into the house, and she knew that the fleeting physical contact was an attempt to re-establish diplomatic relations.

She followed him as he crossed the room to the telephone. It was on the breakfast bar that partitioned off the kitchen from the dining alcove, which in turn was separated from the sitting-room by an ornamental low brick wall. Mark hoisted himself on to the breakfast bar as he picked up the phone. Joyce stood by the wall.

'Rainford,' he said, glancing across at Joyce as he spoke.

She smiled at him. Whatever happened, it had to be better to speak to him calmly, rationally – not to throw the subject into the ring to take its chances with routine grievances. He smiled back, a little sheepishly.

'Oh yes,' he said into the phone. 'It's all right, Frankie, we're remembering. I fully expected rain, of course.' He laughed, as he listened to what Frankie was saying. 'No! I didn't mean that – I just meant that I'm on lawn fatigues, and I had thought I'd get out of it.'

Joyce sat down.

'Right you are, Frankie. See you, love.' He replaced the

receiver. 'Frankie,' he informed Joyce, unnecessarily. 'Reminding us about tonight.

Joyce needed no reminding. She looked at Mark from under her eyelashes, a reproachful, slightly speculative look. 'Are you actually going to come?' she asked.

'Of course.'

But there was no of course about it. He knew that as well as she did, though he wouldn't admit it, not even to himself.

2

Frankie O'Brien replaced the receiver and sat down at the dressing table. She had soft, straight chestnut hair to her collar, clear green eyes, and freckles, if you looked closely. She was looking closely, and without enthusiasm, at her reflection. She was slightly built, seeming almost fragile in the tight jeans which accentuated her thin legs, but that was deceptive. Frankie had little time for fragility.

Richard Hascombe sat on the end of the bed, putting on his shoes. 'I expect your secret is out,' he said.

She could see his reflection, smiling at her. Perhaps even laughing at her a little. He had a strong face, with mobile, pleasing features. They pleased her anyway. She smiled back, turning to face him. They had met three months previously at the Blakes', but it had taken him two months to ask her out to dinner. So he should laugh.

'A little ironic,' he said, 'under the circumstances.'

'I liked the circumstances,' she answered with a smile.

She had not meant to stay last night, but they had eaten too well, and drunk too well, and talked too far into the night to do anything other than fall into bed and sleep. Until last night, she had jealously guarded their infant relationship from the inevitable advice and possible disapproval of their mutual friends. And until last night they had not shared a bed with the sole intention of sleeping in it. To Frankie, it had seemed all the more intimate for that.

'One night of unbridled sleep, and you'll be the talk of the

14

village,' he said. 'It doesn't seem fair to me.' He went to the wardrobe to select a tie.

'Sylvia will be rehearsing her speech,' Frankie said, her tone much more cheerful than she felt. Sylvia Blake knew her better than anyone had a right to, and she had already received thoughtful glances.

'Youth cannot mate with age?' he said, only half in fun. 'She might be right, Frankie.'

Frankie shrugged. 'And Alan will think I must want to spend your money,' she said.

'I might be after yours. What's this I hear about a legacy?'

Frankie stiffened.

'Can I ask you about that?'

She could feel the dread already, and she turned quickly back to the mirror. If she kept busy, perhaps this time she wouldn't make a fool of herself. 'You can ask me anything you like,' she said, her voice a little hoarse. She opened her powder compact, and her hand shook.

'Houses, isn't it?'

She dabbed on face-powder, then removed most of it with a tissue. 'A couple of two-up, two-downs with sitting tenants,' she said. 'My father left me them, and some money.' There, she thought. You've made it. She smiled a liberally lipsticked smile at him, then kissed the lipstick off on the tissue.

'What did your father do?'

She smeared green eye-shadow on to one eyelid. 'This and that,' she said. 'Originally, he was a bricklayer.' She found a piece of the tissue that hadn't yet been used, and took off most of the eye-shadow.

Richard looked into the mirror. 'Why don't you just use less in the first place?' he asked.

'I'm Irish,' she said.

'What was "this and that"?'

She could feel her stomach twisting. 'He bought cheap terraced houses and did them up for sale,' she answered, switching her attention to her other eye. 'A sort of second-hand house dealer,' she added, with what she hoped sounded like a laugh. 'I was fifteen when he died.' The words were coming in a rush,

15

rehearsed and rehearsed.

'And now Mark Rainford looks after them for you?' he asked, his voice disbelieving.

'Yes.'

'Isn't he rather an odd choice? I've only met him once, but from what I hear . . .' he allowed the half-finished sentence to hang in the air.

'Mark's all right,' she said defensively.

'That's not what I've heard.' There was a moment when their eyes met in the glass, and he held up his hands.

'Sorry. Nothing to do with me.'

'No,' she said.

For the first time, there was an awkward silence. It was Frankie who felt obliged to break it.

'Alan Blake and Mark were my trustees,' she said. 'Until I was twenty-one.'

'Did Mark gamble in those days?' Richard asked.

'Not like now,' she conceded. 'He would have a bet – that's what my father liked about him, I think.' She widened her eyes as she brushed on mascara. 'It was one of the reasons he asked him to do it. And Mark was his accountant, anyway.'

'But when you were twenty-one,' Richard persisted. 'What made you ask him to look after them?'

Frankie took a deep breath. 'I didn't want to do it myself. Mark does everything – that's how I want it.'

'But surely Alan Blake would have been a better bet? If you'll pardon the expression,' he added with a quick laugh.

'No.' She moved on to her left eye.

'Blake seems to know you very well,' he said. Frankie swivelled the seat round. 'Yes,' she said, seeing a look in his eyes that she hadn't expected. 'I've worked for him for almost ten years.'

He took a jacket from the wardrobe. 'Frankie,' he said, not looking at her. 'What exactly –?' he broke off. 'No,' he said. 'It's none of my business.'

'Go on,' she said.

He bent down to see himself in the mirror, picking up a hairbrush. 'Have I walked into the middle of something?' He made totally unnecessary passes at his hair.

16

'What do you mean?' she asked, puzzled.

'Between you and Blake.'

'What?' The idea was preposterous. She laughed, glad of the light relief. 'Of course not! What on earth made you think that?'

'It doesn't matter.' He turned up the shirt collar and draped the tie round his neck.

'Richard?' She looked up at him. 'I don't know what you've heard, but that at least isn't true.' She caught the ends of his tie and pulled him down to her, kissing him briefly. 'I don't even like him.'

'That isn't always a bar,' he pointed out, knotting his tie with great care.

'I suppose not,' she said.

'You don't really treat him like your employer,' he said.

'No, I don't suppose I do.' Frankie picked up his hairbrush and sat down again at the dressing table. She'd have to try to explain. 'Sylvia looked after me when my father took ill,' she said. 'That's why I know Alan so well. The Blakes are like family.'

Richard looked surprised. He frowned a little. 'I see. How long have you known them?'

'I've known Sylvia since I was ten.'

Richard pulled up a chair and sat beside her. 'I didn't realise,' he said.

Frankie had a brief, almost impressionistic image of her father that would sweep into her mind and away whenever she thought of him as he was then. Tall, which he wasn't, but he was to a ten-year-old. Broad and muscular, which he had been. Laughing, picking her up to throw her in the air and catch her. But then it would be replaced by the real memories, the ones that didn't evaporate, would never evaporate.

'I was shunted about here and there while he was in hospital,' she said, and she could feel the tears, hot behind her eyes. 'He came home, but he never really got better. Just good and bad days. He couldn't look after me all by himself any more.' She got up and sat on the bed, feeling under it for her sandals to give herself something to do. 'He advertised for someone to come and look after me. Us, in the end,' she said, finding the sandals and unbuckling them unnecessarily to prolong the activity. 'Sylvia

17

came.' The sandals were on and buckled, and she had nothing else to do.

'That seems an odd sort of job for Sylvia,' Richard said.

'Well, David was just a baby,' Frankie explained. 'She wanted to work somewhere she could have him with her.'

Richard looked puzzled. 'What was Blake doing?' he asked.

'Sylvia was married before,' Frankie said. 'All I know about him is that his name was Newman. It broke up when David was about six months old. So it suited Sylvia to work for us.'

'Did she live with you?'

'Not to start with, but he –' The tears were refusing to be blinked back and they blurred her vision. She blew her nose. 'He had more heart attacks, and he went back to hospital. She came then. To stay with us, I mean.' She tried desperately not to cry. 'I would be about thirteen.'

Richard was at her side. 'Don't, Frankie,' he said. 'I'm sorry. I shouldn't have asked.'

'Why not?' She was determined to get to the end of the story so that she wouldn't have to face it again. 'He couldn't do anything much. Mark did it all. But he had a lot of houses at one point, and Mark couldn't do it and his own work. And there wasn't enough income to pay someone else to do it. So,' she said, seeing the finishing post in sight, 'he kept the ones he thought might be an investment and sold the rest as one lot. Alan Blake bought them, and that's how he met Sylvia.' She wiped away the tears, smearing mascara. 'My father was very ill by then. Sylvia coped with him – I don't know how. I was no help.'

'How old were you?' he asked gently.

'Fourteen.' Fourteen, full of adolescent arrogance; fourteen, old enough to know better. Fourteen, and taking advantage of his weakness to do as she pleased. Sylvia, tied to the house by an invalid and a six-year-old, couldn't stop her. 'Sylvia stayed after he died,' she said. 'When I was eighteen, she married Alan. By that time I was working for him. I think Sylvia made him give me a job.' She glanced up at him.

'Would you mind very much going away for a minute? Please?'

He left, closing the door quietly, and she allowed herself the tears without the embarrassment of an audience.

3

Sylvia Blake washed and David dried. Alan had come back from the golf club and they had eaten a silent lunch; now he was in the study, ostentatiously awaiting a phone-call. Mrs Mac didn't come at weekends, so Sylvia shared the chores with her son. They both rather enjoyed their weekends, when they could take life at their pace, and not at Alan's, whose life moved to the beat of a much more strident drum than did theirs. Alan, Sylvia thought, was rather like an artist's impression of the man who has everything; he had constantly groomed executive-grey hair, manicured hands, a Mercedes and an expensive, well-appointed house.

But he also had a business with severe cash-flow problems, appearances to keep up and a marriage which was crumbling under the strain. The increased frequency of the rows, and the almost casual violence which attended them, was making it difficult to keep up those appearances, when appearances were all they had. Pretence was the only shared experience they had left; it was what the marriage had really always been about. In its own unlikely way, the Blakes' union had been a success, and as long as Sylvia could paper over the cracks, she would.

She smiled at David, who was as different from Alan as it was possible to be. David's sole ambition was to paint, and time hardly mattered if he was engrossed in what he was doing. The ability to draw which had impressed Alan when David was eight, and a brand new stepson, merely irritated him now, and he regarded the whole thing as a waste of time and opportunity. But David had never sought Alan's approval of anything he did, and his stepfather's occasional assertions that he should be putting his energies into something more profitable had no effect on him whatsoever.

Sylvia had never been able to draw anything much more than matchstick men, but she understood David's passion. She worried a little because he was so sure he could earn a living that way, and that seemed to her unlikely, however good he was. His art teacher assured her that he was good enough to go to art college, provided he accepted their tuition and didn't think he was Van Gogh. Sylvia was inclined to think that he did and pointed out to him from time to time that Van Gogh didn't get luncheon vouchers. He ought to be preparing for the exam, but he wasn't. He was working on something of his own, every minute he could, in the studio above the kitchen that had once been two servants' rooms. Alan had reluctantly agreed to the conversion, complaining that it cost so much they might as well have had the two servants.

'Why don't you come this evening?' she asked.

'I might come later,' David said. 'But I want to go out first.'

Out meant sketching. Not a disco, or the cinema, or a girlfriend. It meant that he would go off somewhere on his own with his sketch pad and his camera.

'Frankie will be there,' Sylvia said, encouragingly. David had had a crush on Frankie since he was ten. She might serve as bait to get him to do something a little more sociable than usual. 'And you could give Kim a ring – she might like to come.' Kim was the fifteen-year-old daughter of friends. Sylvia harboured a hope that her charms might help to take David out of himself.

He shook his head. 'She wouldn't,' he said. 'She thinks I'm too young for her.'

They laughed. The phone rang and was answered immediately. It was a reminder of Alan's presence in the house, and David's expression changed immediately. He returned to the plate-drying.

It was a short conversation; the bell on the kitchen extension tinkled as Alan hung up. A few minutes later, he appeared in the kitchen, announcing that he was going out. The front door banged, the garage door whined open, the Mercedes crunched over the gravel, and he was gone.

David cheered up instantly. Sylvia wished that they would try to get on with one another, but it was a forlorn hope.

4

Richard knocked on the door, and opened it cautiously.

Frankie had stopped crying and was obviously angry with herself for having allowed her emotions to escape. She turned away from him, still struggling to push the inconvenient things back into their box and shut the lid.

'Why does it still upset you so much?' he asked, in a deliberate sabotage attempt. It was the closest he had been; he didn't want to lose her.

'He worried about me,' she said, her voice flat. 'All the time.'

'Parents do worry about their children.' He sat beside her on the bed. He had known that Frankie's mother had died in a road accident when Frankie was too young to remember; he had had no idea about the rest. He received a sideways, suspicious look.

'They don't all have as much cause,' she said, her hair falling across her face as she looked away again. 'He was so ill.'

'That wasn't your fault.'

'No. But I just ran wild because they couldn't stop me. I hurt him – I know I did.'

Richard brushed the dark red hair away from her eyes. 'You were a child,' he said. 'You're blaming yourself for having been a child.' He let her hair fall back, and she hid behind it once more.

'Everyone feels guilty, you know,' he said, determined to comfort her. 'Whenever someone that close to you dies, you feel you could have done more, said more. Said less, come to that,' he added, and she looked up quickly.

'I do know what it's like,' he said. 'My wife was ill. Not for as long as your father, but long enough for me to do all the right things. I didn't, of course. No-one ever does. And they shouldn't, because it would be false.'

Frankie allowed her hand to be held.

'If you had stayed at home and read to him every night, you wouldn't have been his daughter. It would have been a calculated move, like a death-bed conversion.'

The smile was involuntary, prompted by a sudden memory of her father on that very subject. 'You should have heard him about that,' she said. 'He hated people who saw the light because they were knocking on a bit.' She laughed, a little shakily. 'He called them lapsed atheists. "Please God, don't let me get religion!" he used to say.'

Richard laughed with her. 'And I take it he didn't suffer a conversion?'

'Not him. A staunch atheist to the end.'

'Then he'd hardly be expecting one from you, would he?'

She shrugged a little and moved to the dressing table to repair her make-up.

'Why don't you like Blake?' he asked.

'Do you?'

'I don't know him very well.' He had to be careful of what he said. 'Has he . . . ?' He searched for the words. 'Has he hurt you in some way?'

'Hurt me?' Her eyes shone slightly. 'How could he have done that?' Her voice was sharp, her cheeks slightly pink.

'I don't know,' he answered. 'You tell me.'

She didn't respond.

'You don't think your father got a fair deal over the property he sold to Blake, do you?'

Frankie raised an eyebrow. 'You've been doing your homework all right,' she said.

Richard shook his head. 'That's all I know,' he said. 'That Blake bought some property from your father and that you weren't very happy. No more than that, honestly.' He smiled. 'And I wasn't prying – somebody just happened to tell me.'

'Since you ask,' she said, 'I don't think anyone's ever had a fair deal from Alan Blake. Why are you so interested in him anyway?'

'I had a decision to make,' he said. 'And it could affect you in more ways than one. I wanted to know how you felt about him.'

'A decision about Alan? It must be money, then.' She stood up. 'Right?'

'Right first time.' He put out a hand to take hers, but she turned towards the window. He couldn't be sure whether she'd done it deliberately or not.

He joined her and pointed towards the wood at the bottom of the garden. 'You can take a short cut through there,' he said. 'To the old quarry.'

Frankie smiled. 'Why would I want to do that?' she asked.

'I go there sometimes. It's like being on the moon, or something. Helps you get things in perspective.'

The green eyes rested on his for a moment, then moved back to the window. 'Maybe,' she said. 'But it doesn't make them go away, does it?'

'Probably not.' Richard abandoned his attempt at amateur psychology. He looked up at the sky. 'Do you think it's going to stay like this?' he asked. 'Or will there be a cloudburst as soon as I get the barbecue going?'

Frankie frowned slightly. 'Do you wish you'd never let yourself in for all of this?'

Richard smiled. Tonight was a rather belated housewarming, suggested by Alan Blake as a way of meeting the neighbours; Sylvia had advised on the invitations, and Frankie had talked him into making it a barbecue, of all things, after he had carelessly boasted of his skill with a hamburger. Yes, he wished he'd never let himself in for it. But Frankie was looking forward to it.

'Of course I don't,' he said stoutly. 'It should be fun.'

5

Joyce looked at the television; not at the screen, not at the silent horses streaking along the straight, but at the piece of furniture, at the twenty-six-inch colour set with cabinet. At the video recorder, at the hi-fi.

Two horses passed the winning post and the crowds erupted in soundless appreciation. Now, she saw the images, the garish colours, the steam rising from the horse as the saddle was removed, the slaps on the back for the owner, on the neck for the animal. She snapped the switch and she was no longer part of their perspiring, pernicious world.

She jumped when she heard Mark's key in the lock.

'Joyce! Joyce!' Mark's voice was urgent.

Joyce ran to the door, her heart in her mouth. 'What is it? What's wrong?' she cried.

Mark stood in the hallway, his hands full of ten-pound notes, grinning from ear to ear. 'Look at this!' he shouted, throwing the notes into the air and planting a kiss on her lips while the money fluttered to the ground.

Joyce just looked at him, at his eyes shining with elation and triumph.

'You promised,' she said. 'You promised you weren't going to go to the betting shop.'

'Four hundred and twenty pounds! Count it!' he yelled. He squatted down and began picking up notes.

'Mark,' she said. 'If you don't stop this, I'm leaving you.'

He looked up, half-laughing.

'I can't live like this,' she said and knelt down beside him. 'You've got to tell me everything. Tell me the truth. And tell me *now*.'

'I've won some money,' he said, looking bewildered. 'What else is there to tell?'

'How much do we *owe*?' she shouted. 'Because we're paying it back. Every penny.'

'What do you mean? We don't owe anything.' Mark picked up the money and followed her into the living-room. 'Honestly, you don't have to worry,' he said.

Joyce walked into the kitchen, still pursued by Mark. She filled the kettle, because it was something to do.

He waved the money under her nose. 'It's for you,' he said.

'Stop it,' she begged him, close to tears, pushing away the money as she walked past him to the cupboard. 'Don't!' She took out tea and dropped two teabags into the pot, barely aware of what she was doing.

The small kitchen filled with steam from the kettle and she filled the teapot, splashing little pinpricks of boiling water on her arm.

'Can't I have a bet in peace? What harm's it ever done you?'

'It's you,' she said. 'It's harming you.'

'How? How has it harmed me?'

Joyce banged two mugs on the table. 'You can't *stop*!'

'Don't be ridiculous! Thank God I don't drink much – you'd have me down as an alcoholic.'

'It's just as bad.'

'What? Have you ever suffered?'

Joyce began pouring the tea that neither of them wanted. 'It's an addiction,' she said.

'Addiction? Look – it's what I do to relax, that's all.' He smiled. 'Joyce – you take it far too seriously.' He took his tea through to the coffee table, switched on the television and sat down.

Joyce went after him, and before she had time to think twice, snatched the paper out of his hands. 'Tell me the truth,' she demanded.

The thin, dark face that looked up at her was impassive, expressionless. 'What truth?' he asked.

'Mark, you've got to tell me the truth. Don't you understand?'

He took her hand and pulled her gently down beside him. 'You shouldn't get so upset,' he said. 'There's no need. Everything's fine.' He put his arm round her.

'I'm frightened,' she said.

'What of?' He drew her closer. 'There's nothing to be frightened of.' He was kissing her hair, her eyes. Gentle, comforting kisses. Joyce jumped up again, away from him.

'I know all about it, Mark.' She was plunging in at the deep end. That wasn't like any of the opening gambits she'd rehearsed during sleepless nights. They had been carefully worded; they had been by turns compassionate, indignant, angry. They hadn't consisted of a bald statement.

Mark froze, his teacup at his lips, for the tiniest of moments before he carried on. 'What do you know?' he asked, his voice artificially light and careless.

She switched off the television again. 'I know how you can gamble away so much money, and still pay for things like this.' She closed the cabinet door.

'I win,' he said airily, picking up a handful of notes. 'There's no mystery. I win.'

'No, you don't.' She walked over and looked down at him. 'You've won today, that's all. But you don't really win. You lose, like everyone else. The bookies win.' She dropped to her knees beside him. 'You can't pretend any more,' she said. 'Not any more.'

Chapter Two

1

Richard watched Frankie as she set up her tape-recorder. It was her pride and joy and had more buttons and lights than the Concorde flight deck. It was a complete mystery to him. She had spent days recording bits and pieces of both their record collections and was now threading through a tape that she assured him would give three hours of continuous music to the guests. She had attempted to give him instructions on how to turn it to give another three hours, but both the instructions and the idea appalled him.

'I've just put on a mixture,' she was saying. 'Mostly old pop records – is that all right? It won't really sound all that great because it's recorded at the slow speed, but I thought that probably wouldn't matter since people won't really be listening anyway.'

'It'll sound all right to me,' he said.

'I've tried to put on things that they can dance to if they want,' she continued, straightening up from her labours. 'After all – what's the point in having a paved terrace unless it's danced on?'

He grinned. 'You'd be happier if I suddenly went bust, wouldn't you? We could live in trendy poverty in your house, and grow marijuana in the window box.'

'I don't even *have* a window box,' she said.

He opened the French windows on to the terrace. 'Go on – look,' he said. 'Isn't that better than looking out at Brampton High Street?'

'I like Brampton High Street.' Frankie went out to hook up the speakers in the garden, swearing mildly as the wire became entangled in the burglar alarm. 'And there's another thing I haven't got,' she said, successfully completing the connection and joining him back in the house.

'Pleasant situation,' Richard said. 'Extensive grounds, part woodland, with summerhouse. Interested?'

Frankie shook her head. 'I need to have my own house,' she said.

'This would be your own house.'

'No, it wouldn't. It would be your house. At best it would be our house, and I need somewhere of my own. Somewhere I know I can go, if I want to.' She smiled. 'I'll stay with you as long as you like,' she said. 'But I won't live with you, and I'll never make any promises.'

Richard laughed. 'You are Irish, aren't you?'

He wished no-one was coming. As the thought crossed his mind, the door bell rang.

'This is it, chaps,' he said, stubbing out his cigar, as the pendulum clock whirred into action and softly chimed the half-hour.

'Why does *someone* always insist on coming early?' Frankie asked.

'They'll be the last to leave – you'll see,' Richard said. 'Are all systems go?'

Frankie pressed one of the buttons and guitars strummed gently in the garden. 'Affirmative,' she replied, kissing him on the cheek. 'Go and meet your guests.'

2

Mark had meant to keep his word; he really had, he told himself. It was just that he'd lost a bit more than he'd meant to, and there was an evening meeting at Westbridge dog track. He had worked out that he could get there for the first race or two and still be back in time to change and be at Hascombe's by eight. Frankie had said any time from seven, so that would be all right. Anyway, the time didn't matter – it wasn't as though it was a dinner party. He'd just stay for the next race, and then go. If Joyce still wanted to pop into Hascombe's for a little while, they could go for an hour or so. He hoped she didn't – he felt far from sociable after his enforced heart-to-heart with her.

3

Alan hadn't returned, and Sylvia, having now made use of her expensive range of cosmetics, was ready, correctly casual in blue jeans and tee shirt, and waiting. Seven o'clock had come and gone, and by seven-fifteen she wrote a note telling Alan that she had gone on alone. David had popped his head round the door to announce that he was going out; she had had one last attempt at persuading him to come, but he had simply said that he might.

She strolled down the road to Richard Hascombe's house, enjoying the feel of the westering sun on her back, the hot dry smell of the summer and the unusual sensation of being herself. She didn't have to be arch and brittle in response to Alan's carefully nurtured male chauvinism, she didn't have to laugh at the jokes that she had heard a thousand times. She could talk to people on her own terms, for a while at least. When she was with Alan, he had a tendency to show people round her, as if she were a vintage car.

The smell of burning charcoal and sizzling food met her as she rounded the side of the house, and she smiled. Smoke drifted gently in the air across the lawn, where knots of people stood talking. They had obviously stayed in the groups they had arrived in, and she wondered how successful it was going to be. She waved at one or two of the neighbours and crossed the grass towards the barbecue itself, and Frankie.

'Sylvia!' Frankie smiled broadly. 'Have a hamburger. *Please* don't say you're not hungry.'

Sylvia was hungry; the short walk had reminded her that it had been some time since lunch. She set about her hamburger with an abandon of which Alan would have heartily disapproved.

'It's gorgeous,' she said, with her mouth full. She swallowed before attempting further conversation. 'What's in it?'

Frankie grinned. 'It's a secret recipe – they're better than the ones you get in Brampton, aren't they?'

'I wouldn't know,' Sylvia said. 'But they're better than mine. Do me another one.'

'Oh, good,' said Frankie delightedly. 'Maybe you'll encourage the others.'

Sylvia glanced over her shoulder. 'Is no-one having anything?' she whispered, looking at the array of food.

'You, me and Richard,' Frankie said. 'We'll get very fat.'

Sylvia laughed at the idea of Frankie getting fat. 'It wouldn't do you any harm,' she said. 'Not that there's the least chance that you will ever put on weight.'

'I don't know what they thought a barbecue was,' Frankie said, building Sylvia's next hamburger. She looked round. 'It's not exactly going with a swing, is it?'

Sylvia chewed thoughtfully, guessing at the flavours. 'Did you invent this recipe?' she asked, suspiciously.

'What do you think?'

'I think you burn cornflakes.'

'I do.' Frankie laughed. 'Richard was in the States, you know, where they know how to do these things properly.' Her eyes twinkled as Richard came into earshot in time to catch her last sentence.

'I'm glad you could make it,' Richard said. 'Perhaps you can liven up the proceedings a little.'

'I'm not the life and soul of many parties,' Sylvia warned him, with a smile.

'What are we doing wrong?' He asked Frankie in a stage whisper.

'Give them time,' Sylvia advised him.

'How long do they need?'

Sylvia laughed. 'About fifteen years.'

'Where's Alan?' Frankie asked.

'Oh – he had to go out this afternoon – he got held up. He asked me to apologise,' she said untruthfully to Richard. 'I'm sure he'll get here as soon as he can.'

As she spoke, Joyce Rainford arrived, looking pink and bothered.

'I've never walked up that hill before,' she said, catching her breath. 'It's harder work than you think, isn't it? I thought I wasn't going to make it, I really did. It must have taken me twenty minutes – isn't that awful?' She accepted a drink, but like everyone else, refused food. 'I might have something later,' she said. 'But I'll have to get my breath back. It's just as well they've put that bench halfway up. . .'

Sylvia nodded and smiled in the right places. Poor Joyce had put her tongue into overdrive again, which she seemed to think would stop people noticing that Mark wasn't there.

'I see you're a grass widow too,' Sylvia said, in an effort to make Joyce see that she wasn't unique in her lack of escort, but it didn't work. She just kept glancing nervously round, in the vain hope that Mark would materialise.

'It's a lovely garden,' Sylvia tried next, as Frankie arrived back with Joyce's drink.

'Isn't it?' Joyce said. 'I've caught glimpses of it from the bus – you can see it from the top deck. I like looking at gardens – they're so restful, aren't they? Of course, ours is tiny, and it's almost impossible to get Mark to do anything, but I do enjoy it. Not that I know anything about it, but you've got to learn, haven't you? Still, I expect Richard's got a gardener, hasn't he?'

'Part-time,' Frankie said. 'Mrs Rogers's husband does it at the weekends.'

'Oh – he doesn't work for Richard full-time?' Joyce asked, seizing the topic.

'No. He's got another job during the week.'

'I see. So it's just Mrs Rogers who really works for him? Full-time, I mean. . .'

Her voice went on and on, and Sylvia cast surreptitious glances round as she responded in accordance with the tone, rather than the words.

Richard had drifted off to talk to his new neighbours; Frankie, like Sylvia, was listening politely to Joyce. Unlike her, she was joining in the conversation. No sign of the errant Mark, nor, come to that, of Alan. As the thought formed, Alan gave the lie to it by appearing suddenly in their midst.

Joyce was still looking petrified – more so, of course, now that Alan had arrived, because now she was the only person there without an escort, and her conversation found yet another gear.

'Alan – I didn't really say thank you properly yesterday. I was in such a rush, but it really was good of you – the buses are

30

practically non-existent, aren't they? When one does come, it's full of people from Westbridge – you'd wonder why they'd want to come into Brampton to shop when Westbridge has got the new centre – have you been there? It really is nice, though I must say it's just the same old shops really – the Boots is enormous, though. You can get almost anything. Oh – and there's a lovely camera shop – you'd like it, I'm sure. There are quite a few shops that specialise – it's got a record shop that says it can get anything. . .'

Sylvia glanced at Frankie.

'You should talk,' Frankie said to Joyce. 'You *work* there, and you still shop in Brampton.'

Joyce laughed, a quick nervous laugh. 'I didn't take an oath of allegiance,' she said.

'All the same,' said Frankie. 'The city fathers wouldn't like to hear an employee running down their shopping centre.'

'It's nice,' Joyce said. 'It really is – have you been there?'

'Once,' Frankie replied. 'They charge too much for parking and I always feel a bit as though I've been in prison when I come out of one of these covered places.'

'A bit too close to home?' Alan asked.

Frankie's smile vanished. She turned away, going towards the house.

Sylvia glared at Alan and caught up with Frankie. 'Where's the bathroom?' she asked. 'I don't think the hamburgers have done much for my lipstick.'

They walked into the house, and Frankie led her to the stairs. 'Third door on the right,' she said. 'Sorry the party's not more fun.'

'I'm enjoying it,' Sylvia said, unconvincingly.

'Liar!' Frankie laughed. Then her face sobered. 'I could murder Mark, you know. I rang him up specially, so that he'd know he was expected to turn up.'

'Poor Joyce,' said Sylvia. 'She will try covering up for him. He doesn't seem to understand what he's doing to her.' She went upstairs to find the third door on the right.

Her lipstick re-applied, she lingered in the cool near-darkness of the shaded bathroom, away from Joyce's chatter and Alan's

31

malevolence. Her eye roved along the shelf and it didn't take Sherlock Holmes to work out who owned the other toothbrush, a recent acquisition, whose discarded wrapping was still on the shelf. Frankie was so untidy.

4

Frankie watched from the sitting-room doorway as Richard flicked a switch, and the garden was dotted with the fairy lights which had been distributed on various bushes and trees.

'Nice,' she said, trying hard to forget what Alan had said. She would just have to try to keep out of his way.

'Is it too early, do you think?' he asked her.

'No – it's almost twenty to eight,' she said. 'That's evening, isn't it?'

He smiled as she slipped her arms round his waist. 'Have you been to a worse party?' he asked.

'Yes,' she said decidedly.

'How could it possibly have been worse?'

'You weren't there.'

'So now I'm your straight man,' Richard said, smiling. 'I suppose we'd better mingle. No-one else is.'

'Do you mind if I don't, for a moment?' she asked.

'I thought there was something wrong,' he said. 'What's happened?'

Frankie wished that she could just sometimes assume Mark Rainford's look of complete indifference.

'Nothing,' she said. 'I've just mingled with the wrong people, that's all. I'd like to keep out of the way for a minute or two.'

'You're excused,' he said, kissing her and walking out purposefully to play the host.

'Well, well.'

Frankie turned sharply to see Alan Blake in the doorway.

'Isn't that nice?' he said. 'You've made a new friend.'

5

Sylvia was still thinking about Frankie as she came downstairs. The sound of Alan's voice made her stop. For a second or two, she didn't know what he was talking about, but then he made himself crystal clear. She couldn't see because of the curve of the stairs, but there was only one person to whom he could be speaking. She heard Frankie's angry reply as she hurried down.

She found Alan on his own at the foot of the stairs. 'What do you think you're doing?' she asked.

6

Joyce, abandoned first by Frankie and Sylvia and then by Alan, had walked away from the other guests to the bottom of the garden. There she had wandered along the path leading into the wood and found a little summerhouse, and solitude.

She had closed the door on the determinedly cheerful music and allowed herself some respite from her self-imposed, fixed-smile torture. But then the thought that Mark might turn up while she was out of sight began to worry her and, reluctantly, she walked back to the garden.

She found a seat by the edge of the wood where she could watch for Mark's arrival without being too involved.

'Hello.' Frankie's voice made her jump. She looked up to see her standing beside her, her hands thrust into her pockets. 'Would you like another drink?'

'No,' she said quickly. 'I'm fine.'

Frankie flopped down beside her, hooking one thin, blue-jeaned leg over the other. Why didn't she just tell Frankie? She knew why, of course. Because she was afraid of Frankie's reaction and she didn't trust Mark's assurances.

'Do you think we should organise some games or something?' Frankie was asking, with a grin. 'Would that work?'

Joyce managed a smile, looking around at the sober citizens of

Long Caswell. 'I don't think they'll go much for musical chairs,' she said. She wasn't gabbling, as she usually did when she was nervous; there was never any desire to talk Frankie away. Even now, even in this mess, she didn't feel obliged to fill the spaces with words.

'How about Hunt the Nubile Nude?' Frankie suggested. 'Do us a favour – strip off and hide in the wood.' She leant back on the bench, her eyes closed.

'I'm never sure what nubile actually means,' Joyce said. 'But I'd be no good unless it means overweight.' She took a deep breath and glanced at Frankie, who was still in the same attitude, her head back, her eyes closed. 'Frankie,' she said, her heart plunging with the effort of the first sentence, still only half-formulated.

But it was wasted effort, because Frankie's eyes snapped open, impossibly green in the pale evening light. 'Oh God,' she moaned dramatically, 'here comes Mrs Milray.'

Joyce looked up to see one of Richard's exquisitely groomed middle-aged guests bearing down on them.

'Frances, dear,' the visitor said, as she approached. 'I had no idea *you* were here!'

Not much, thought Joyce.

Frankie had uncrossed her legs, and was sitting up straight, like a child in school. 'Mrs Milray,' she said. 'Do you know Joyce Rainford?'

'No,' beamed Mrs Milray. 'I don't believe we've met.' She extended a hand to Joyce, regarding her closely. 'And yet you seem somehow familiar,' she added.

'How do you do,' Joyce said.

'Well, Frances – I didn't know that you were a friend of the Hascombes,' she said. 'Have you known them long?'

Joyce looked quickly at Frankie.

'Them?' Frankie was saying. 'I'm afraid I only know Richard.'

Mrs Milray's face was registering its social gaffe expression. 'Oh, do forgive me. You haven't met his daughter, I take it?'

Joyce could see that Frankie was lost; so, unfortunately, could Mrs Milray. Frankie wore her heart on her sleeve – there was no mistaking her reactions to anything.

34

'Didn't you know that he had a daughter?' Mrs Milray was asking, with an air of innocence quite at odds with her quick, observant eyes. These were flashed for an instant at Joyce, to see what she knew. But Joyce had learned from Mark the trick of bluffing. She smiled almost encouragingly at Mrs Milray.

Frankie said nothing.

'Don't you find him a most interesting man? He's done so much,' Mrs Milray said.

And made so much money doing it, Joyce thought, but she didn't speak. If she had, she might have informed Mrs Milray that Frankie was no more interested in Richard Hascombe's money than she was in nuclear physics, and Frankie might not have thanked her. Still, it was giving Joyce a little light relief from her own problems to watch Mrs Milray making preliminary passes at the bull.

The bull, however, was refusing to snort and paw the ground and provide Mrs Milray with her sport. Frankie merely smiled. 'Yes, he is,' she agreed, mildly.

Mrs Milray paused for a moment, then thrust another goad into Frankie's none-too-tough hide. 'They say he might be on the New Year's Honours List,' she said, conversationally.

'Honours List?' Frankie's eyes opened wide.

'He's very highly thought of in the City,' Mrs Milray assured her. 'But one musn't count one's chickens!'

Joyce cleared her throat. 'I thought these things were kept secret,' she said.

'Oh, they are – but one hears rumours.'

I'll bet one does, thought Joyce, uncharitably. I'll bet one starts a few as well.

'I think some people were quite surprised that he wasn't in the Birthday Honours,' Mrs Milray went on. 'I'm certain that he should have been.'

Frankie looked distinctly uncomfortable, as well she might with Mrs Milray's darts lodged in her, but she was still being as meek as a lamb.

'You'd meet Mr Hascombe through the Blakes, I expect?'

'Yes,' Frankie answered.

Mrs Milray nodded. 'Mrs Blake really has been very good to

you, hasn't she?'

Frankie dropped her eyes. 'Yes,' she agreed.

'I don't really know Mr Blake at all,' Mrs Milray admitted.

Alan's business must be in a bad way, Joyce thought. One would never disown one of the town's biggest employers unless one had heard rumours that he was going bust. And recently, Alan had hinted as much himself. She wished she could remember where she'd met Mrs Milray, because she had. She was sure of it.

'I believe Mr Hascombe may be joining Blake's board?'

'I wouldn't know, Mrs Milray.'

'Ah!' Mrs Milray laughed prettily. 'Keeping secrets. And you're quite right. But you know, dear, it isn't always wise. Not always.'

Mrs Milray was beginning to sound desperate, Joyce thought. Worse by far than being gored was having the bull ignore one's flourishes with the cape.

'So you haven't met Amanda?' she said.

Joyce took a squint at Frankie, who was beginning to look perpetually bewildered.

'Amanda?'

'Mr Hascombe's daughter. She'd be – let me see now.' Her eyes screwed up to indicate how difficult it was to dredge up details of this sort. 'She'd be about your age, dear.'

Mrs Milray sat down, sandwiching Frankie's slight frame between her own and Joyce's. She breathed in the soft summer evening air.

'Yes', she said. 'Just about your age.'

7

Richard wanted to talk to Sylvia; perhaps he could ask her to dance.

He looked round, but he couldn't see either her or Blake. Perhaps they'd given up on the festivities and gone home. He wanted a drink, and the whisky bottle was empty. Picking it up, he walked back into the house. If this was getting to know the neighbours, he would sooner be a recluse. It wasn't until he was in the sitting-room that he heard what was going on; outside, the music had masked the sounds. He ran down the corridor between the sitting-room and the kitchen and threw open the door.

Blake, his hand raised to strike another blow, turned and froze, like some sort of ugly action-still. Sylvia, backed against the wall, still protected her face with her arms.

'Get out,' Richard said, his voice quiet, more from shock than for effect.

Blake lowered his hand, but didn't move.

'Get *out*,' Richard repeated.

Blake strode towards the door and banged it shut behind him. Richard expelled his breath and walked over to the hatch between the kitchen and the corridor to the sitting-room. Closing over the hatch, he turned to Sylvia.

Her lip was bleeding. He dampened a cloth and handed it to her silently, looking at the damage Blake had done, at the angry marks on her face and arms. He hated to think what might have happened if he hadn't wanted a Scotch.

'Do you need a doctor?' he asked.

She shook her head. 'No, thank you,' she said with difficulty. She walked slowly to the sink and rinsed out the cloth. 'It's not that bad.'

'Does he make a habit of this?' Richard asked.

She didn't answer, but her body language was eloquent enough. 'Don't tell anyone,' she said, when finally she did speak. 'Please. Don't tell Frankie. Don't tell her *anything*, please.'

Richard agreed without thinking. He nodded. 'But I still think you should let a doctor have a look at you.'

'No, it's all right.' She even smiled. 'If I could just clean up a bit.'

He stood aside, expecting her to go up to the bathroom. Instead, she washed her face at the sink. He handed her a towel.

'I don't want anyone to see me,' she said, patting her face gingerly. 'I know you can't understand. Thank you for not trying to.'

He reached into the cupboard for the whisky he'd come in for and two glasses. Without asking, he poured her one as well. 'All the same,' he said. 'I'd like to.'

8

Mrs Milray was never going to go away, Frankie had decided. They were all going to be here for the rest of their lives, she instinctively parrying the thrusts of Mrs Milray's innocent, wide-eyed questioning. Every now and then her conversation had included Joyce, and Frankie had no doubt that it would be loaded with significance, but you couldn't tell from Joyce's response. Joyce could take on any number of Mrs Milrays and win, because they gave her something to fight. It was Mark, easy-going, laid-back Mark who had the whip hand with Joyce. She had told Frankie once that it was like trying to have a row with a blancmange. And when he did what he had done tonight, and failed yet again to turn up, then Joyce would lose her nerve. But give her someone like Mrs Milray, and she would find it again.

But now even Joyce, who could say more words per minute than anyone Frankie knew, had lapsed into a kind of stunned silence under Mrs Milray's interrogation.

'Frankie?' Joyce asked suddenly. 'Could you run me home do you think? I really don't feel very well.'

Frankie had no idea whether it was a diplomatic lie or the unvarnished truth but, either way, she was intensely grateful to Joyce.

'Of course,' she said, jumping up. 'I'll just go and let Richard know. I'll take you to the car.' She smiled at Mrs Milray. 'Do excuse me, Mrs Milray – it was very nice seeing you again.'

'And you, dear,' said Mrs Milray. 'And I do hope you feel better soon,' she added, to Joyce.

'Thank you.'

Frankie and Joyce walked back up the garden, crossing to the pathway by the border of the lawn, where the stock was beginning to perfume the evening air.

'Well,' Joyce said. 'You're distracting him from his serious business, you're young enough to be his daughter and you've somehow queered his pitch with Buckingham Palace. Not bad for an evening's work.'

Frankie smiled, but she found it far from funny.

'Oh Frankie!' Joyce said. 'You're not taking that old witch seriously? She's jealous! Is there a Mr Milray?'

Frankie shook her head.

'She probably ate him,' Joyce said, as they squeezed past Alan Blake's car, parked at the side of the house.

Trust Alan, Frankie thought, to find the most inconvenient place to leave his car. Her eye was caught by a file on the passenger seat. Mrs Milray seemed to know all about Richard's possible investment in Blake's, when she had heard about it for the first time during her unpleasant encounter with Alan. Perhaps the file could tell her more.

'There you are,' she said to Joyce, as she unlocked her car. 'You wait here – I won't be a moment.' She turned away, and then back. 'It was true, was it? About your not feeling well?'

'It's true that I'd like to go home,' Joyce said.

Frankie laughed and walked back through the narrow gap between the greenhouse and Alan's car, looking again at the file on the front seat. No-one could see her here. On an impulse, she tried the passenger door but, rather to her relief, it was locked. For one thing, snooping was snooping, and for another, she might have got caught.

She went into the house, having failed to see Richard from the vantage point of the terrace, and went down the dark corridor to the kitchen. The door opened and Richard almost sidled out.

'Frankie?' he said. 'Are you looking for me?'

There was something very odd about him, Frankie thought. He looked as though he'd been caught stealing the spoons.

'I'm taking Joyce home,' she said. 'She's obviously given up on Mark.' She smiled briefly and gave him a quick perfunctory kiss.

'You are coming back?' Richard said.

'I think I might as well go straight home.' She tried to make it sound spontaneous, but it wasn't. Mrs Milray with her talk of Amanda and Honours Lists, had made her feel uncomfortable, especially after what Alan had said. She wanted to go home and think about it.

'But why? Just come back when you've dropped Joyce off. Please.'

'I can't – really,' she said. 'I'll ring you tomorrow.'

'No!' He caught hold of her. 'Don't go.'

'I have to – I can't wear these all weekend – I've got nothing here, Richard.'

'You can pick something up and come back.'

He was holding her by the wrist with no intention of letting go. 'Is this because of Blake?' he asked.

'Alan?' Frankie stared at him. 'What's it got to do with Alan?' She had already answered his ridiculous question about Alan and she was damned if she was going to answer it again.

'Has he been speaking to you?' Richard demanded.

'I don't believe this! You don't seriously think you can dictate who is allowed to speak to me, do you?'

'No, of course not. I didn't mean that.'

'Oh, good! That's all right then,' Frankie said with heavy sarcasm.

'Oh, Frankie!' He sounded irritated; she couldn't really see his face in the windowless corridor. The door of the service hatch was slightly ajar, and the only light they had was from the kitchen, seeping through the crack, revealing fuzzy outlines and no more.

'I can't stay,' she said. 'I want to go home. I need to think.'

'No,' he said again. 'There's nothing to think about.'

9

Perhaps she could ask Frankie in for coffee, Joyce thought, as she waited. If only that awful woman hadn't come, she might have been able to go through with it then, when they were on their own.

Yes, she decided, feeling better for the decision. She'd ask her in and she would speak to her. Mark was so certain.

But then, Mark was usually certain, and often wrong. And almost always lying.

10

'No,' Frankie said. 'I'm not staying.'

'It *is* Blake, isn't it?'

As he spoke, the serving hatch door, caught in a draught from somewhere, swung open a few more inches. The sudden shaft of light caught Frankie's face, pale and angry. Richard glanced over his shoulder to find that the kitchen was now empty. It must have been the back door that had caused the draught, as Sylvia left.

'I won't keep answering that, Richard,' she said.

'No,' he said desperately, turning back to face her. 'I didn't mean it like that – truly, I didn't.'

Her eyes didn't leave his. 'What did you mean?' she asked, her voice hard.

In the prison of the airless, hot corridor, it was hard to believe that there were any other people there. They were caught in a dark, oppressive silence, where the music couldn't be heard. Only its beat, like a pulse, like an aching head. He'd promised not to tell her.

Frankie pushed past him, and almost ran through the sitting-room to the garden. Richard swore to himself, and went after her, calling her. She walked quickly away until she was a safe distance from everyone else, when she stopped abruptly, allowing him to catch up.

His English country garden was dotted with murmuring groups of English country people, consumed no doubt, with English country curiosity, but hiding it well. Frankie swept her hair back from her face, her eyes challenging him to make just one wrong move, an odd splash of fiery drama amid the gentle water colours of her setting. For just an instant, he could understand Ireland's ferocious, bloody history.

He looked round surreptitiously to see who was watching. With consummate skill, the entire garden-party looked away.

'Frankie,' he said urgently. 'Have you seen Blake?'

'Yes,' she said hotly. 'So what?'

'Where is he now?'

'I've no idea. And I'm going. Now.'

Richard thought furiously. Sylvia was gone, Blake was God knew where. 'Look, Frankie – will you stay? Just until I get back?'

'Back? Back from where?'

'There's something I want to do,' he said.

'You do what you like,' she answered. 'I'm not going to be here.'

11

David finished his sketch of the quarry, with the sun heading towards its steep, dangerous edge, casting dark slashes of shadow into its depth. He remembered once trying to explain to Frankie that he sketched objects, but that he painted ideas. The quarry itself might never be in the finished picture, but he wanted to draw it, to recapture the atmosphere. Amid the rape fields, the sudden danger of the quarry, left over from the past, was like anger crossing an otherwise serene face. Frankie's face was what he needed for his picture. He'd seen that look on Frankie's face.

And in an hour, when the sun finally slipped below the quarry's edge, the mood would change again. On the nights when clouds ringed the edges of the sky, its rays shone through them, and a red sunset would turn the sky into a friendly fantasy of islands and inlets. But tonight there was no cloud, and the skies were pale. When the sun went the quarry would grow grey and dark, while above ground would still be light.

Then, it would be a darkened stage, before they dimmed the house-lights.

Chapter Three

1

Frankie and Joyce drove in silence down the Caswells hill, Joyce having heeded Frankie's curt advice not to ask what was wrong.

'Thank you,' Joyce said. She got out and hesitated before closing the door. 'Frankie,' she said. 'Don't let other people spoil it.'

Frankie smiled reluctantly. 'I'm sorry,' she said. 'It's been a difficult evening, what with one thing and another.'

'And don't listen to a word that woman said – she's just jealous.'

Frankie smiled. 'Perhaps. But I don't really think she is. I think she was trying to warn me, somehow.'

'Don't be silly. And since when did you heed warnings?'

Frankie felt grateful for Joyce's low-key attempt to cheer her up, and this time she gave her a real smile. 'I'll see you soon,' she said, and drove off, taking the car out of the Westbridge exit from the Caswells Road and turning at the break in the central reservation. The by-pass provided dual carriageway practically into Brampton itself and on a Saturday night the wide main street was free from its weekday jam of vehicles. She was home by eight thirty-five, home to her own, untidy house – with no domestic staff, no expensive furniture, no private woodland, no lawn to paved terrace at rear.

No Richard. The thought made the house seem just a little chilly. She pulled the paper from the letter box and closed the door. The downstairs rooms had been knocked into one large, open-plan ground floor by her father. The street door opened into it, and the stairs were slightly to the right as you entered. In winter, with an open fire burning, it looked cosy and welcoming. In summer, it tended to have the opposite effect. The kitchen was

43

separate, part of its ceiling sloping under the stairs. She pushed the swing-door and surveyed the untidiness of a kitchen to which she had meant to return yesterday. It was never ship-shape, but even she didn't usually leave it like that, with milk yellowing on the table and bread curling up on the dresser. She spooned coffee into the coffee maker and withdrew. She'd do it later.

The light on the answering machine was lit; she swept the collection of newspapers and magazines from the top and played the tape.

2

Joyce removed her uncomfortably tight clothes and slipped on a pair of old cords and a tee-shirt of Mark's that had seen better days. As she opened the bedroom curtains again, she looked in vain for the comforting sight of Mark's car.

Downstairs, she surveyed the living-room, but even she could find no more surfaces to polish, no more ornaments to straighten. She glanced at the clock. Frankie must be home by now. She would be bound to listen to her telephone messages, and then she would ring, expecting some sort of explanation. Joyce tried to imagine telling her, but her confidence had evaporated at the sight of Frankie's set, angry face, and it had not returned.

And neither, she told herself bitterly, had Mark. So what reliance could she place on his assertions about Frankie? Mark always said what he thought people wanted to hear. He had said that he wasn't gambling any more. He had said that he would be at the barbecue. He had said that it would be all right about Frankie. He even believed what he said, when he was saying it. And Joyce couldn't tell Frankie, not on those grounds. Not on Mark's say-so.

The phone sat there, mocking her, daring her to pick it up when it rang, as it was bound to. She walked over and took the receiver off, laying it on the breakfast bar. But the low hum of the dialling tone seemed to grow louder and louder, filling the whole room, and she couldn't stand that either. She carefully replaced the receiver and looked round almost desperately for something to do, something to help her think. Something to make it possible *not* to answer the phone.

Opening the back door, she stepped out into the cloudless evening. If she wasn't in, she couldn't answer the phone.

3

Frankie sat on the floor as she listened. After a 'Never mind, it can wait' from Alan, Joyce had left no fewer than four messages asking her to ring and a fifth saying that she would see her at the barbecue. And seen her she had, but whatever it was, it must have lost its urgency.

Frankie stared at the tape as though the atmospheric hiss might suddenly launch into a lucid explanation. When it didn't, she leant over and switched it off. She unfolded herself from the floor and dialled Joyce's number. She let it ring for some time before hanging up.

4

'Thank you very much for coming,' Richard said to his last parting guest, but no amount of speeding was going to shift Mrs Milray.

He had got her as far as the gate, but she had turned to face him, determinedly planting herself on the pavement. No longer actually on his property, she clearly had a perfect right to stay there as long as she chose.

'Have you been here long?' she was asking.

'No,' he said. 'This was a sort of house-warming.' He laughed. 'But the house seemed quite warm enough, so I decided the garden would be better.'

'A lovely idea,' Mrs Milray said. 'I should imagine that some of your guests had never seen a hot dog before tonight.'

Richard smiled. 'Some of them did behave a little like High Court judges.'

'Some of them *are* High Court judges,' she said.

'That would explain it.' He glanced up the hill towards the Blakes' house. He could see Blake's Mercedes, but it didn't have much to tell him. 'Perhaps I should make it a more formal affair next time.'

'No!' she said. 'Please don't, Mr Hascombe. They needed reminding that this is the twentieth century.'

He couldn't do anything anyway. The Blakes had presumably gone through this sort of thing before without his riding up on a white charger. He had doubtless over-reacted to the whole thing.

'I think you're going to be good for us, Mr Hascombe,' she said. 'You've seen rather more of the world than the rest of us.'

'Perhaps,' he said. 'But I can't say that I've entirely come to terms with the twentieth century myself. It moves a bit too fast for me.'

She smiled, a sudden, brittle smile. 'Then Frances should be good for you,' she said.

For a moment, he had no idea who Frances was. Then, as he realised, he couldn't believe it. When he'd told Frankie she'd be the talk of the village, he'd thought he was joking.

'Oh,' he said. 'Frankie.' There wasn't much more he could think of to say. Mrs Milray, as his mother would have said, was not backward in coming forward. 'You know Frankie, do you?'

'Indeed, yes.' She smiled again, the same unreal smile. 'So you take good care of her,' she said, her tone archly teasing, her eyes quite serious.

He smiled back. She didn't seem to expect a reply.

'What made you decide on our particular backwater, Mr Hascombe?'

What indeed, thought Richard. Fate. He smiled. 'I was here on business,' he said. 'The Blakes very kindly put me up, and I saw this house. It was for sale and I bought it. As simple as that.'

'How nice,' she said. 'But surely a little far away from London?'

'That's the idea,' he replied. 'But it is possible to commute if you have to. Fortunately, I'm not needed in London for more than three or four days a week.' Why was he telling this woman? 'And I can spend the rest of the time here, writing,' he found himself saying.

'Are you writing a book?' she exclaimed. 'How interesting!'

'I'm afraid it won't top the bestsellers' list,' Richard said. 'It's on currency as a commodity.'

5

Upstairs, pausing only to make her unmade bed, Frankie selected clothes, bundling them into a bag.

She loved her house, loved the independence it gave her, loved the security of being able to close her own front door. But she was damned if she was spending the night alone with the ghosts of the past leering at her when she could be with Richard. Ghosts that Alan had awakened and about which Mrs Milray had warned her.

Surely, surely, all the questions and explanations could wait. How could she have told Richard in that terrible atmosphere of mutual suspicion in which they had found themselves? She would tell him, of course she would. But it would be in circumstances of her own choosing. Unless someone else told him first, of course, which was what Mrs Milray had been suggesting.

She had her coat on when the phone rang. She ran to pick it up before the recorded message answered, sure that it was Richard.

'Frankie? That's you, isn't it?' Alan Blake, his voice hoarse, the words running into one another.

'Yes.'

'Is Sylvia there – is she with you? Is she?'

Frankie's face grew grim. Alan Blake rarely drank and he must have drunk a great deal in an hour to get this bad. 'No, she's not,' she said. 'What's happened?'

'Look, I'm just asking if she's there. That's all. You says she's not. Fine. She's not. Her car's gone. Are you sure she's not there?'

Frankie sighed. 'I've told you she isn't here,' she said.

He shouted something unintelligible above the roar of a jet at his end.

'What?'

'I said that's no guarantee.'

47

6

Mark watched the plane as it climbed. He had actually ducked as it came roaring over, looking as though it would slice the roofs off the houses.

The door was locked and he didn't have his key. He knocked twice, but Joyce obviously wasn't in. She must still be at the barbecue.

Sighing, he got back into the car and drove out of the estate. He didn't feel like going to a party. Blake would be there, for a start, and he didn't think he'd be much good at exchanging small talk with him. But Joyce would never forgive him if he abandoned her at Hascombe's. He drove up the hill, hoping to see Joyce on her way down. But as he signalled and pulled over to Hascombe's house, it was the dreaded Mrs Milray whom he saw, as she walked briskly past the high hedge. Worse yet, Mrs Milray had seen him and was bending to converse with him through the open window.

'Of course!' she said, inexplicably. 'Rainford! I didn't make the connection. I knew I'd seen her somewhere before.'

Mark blinked. 'Sorry?' he said.

'I think I met your wife tonight. Joyce, isn't it?'

'That's right,' Mark said.

'I couldn't think where I'd seen her before. I didn't connect the name at all, but seeing you again – it must be some years since we last met.'

'It must,' Mark agreed.

'You don't live in Brampton any more, do you?' she asked, making it sound a little like an offence to have moved without checking with her first.

'No. We moved here a year or so ago.'

'Here?'

It gave Mark almost a feeling of triumph to tell Mrs Milray something that she didn't already know.

'Well,' he said. 'Not *here* exactly. Lower Caswell. Down with the hoi polloi on the estate.'

'Ah,' she said. 'I can't keep up with the new development. Too many people to keep track of.'

Mark laughed. 'Very trying for you,' he said.

'It is.' She smiled. 'Are you on your way to Mr Hascombe's barbecue?'

'Yes – I'm a bit late,' he said. 'I suppose Joyce isn't very pleased with me.'

Mrs Milray tutted with mock disapproval. 'You're very late,' she said. 'I was the last to leave.'

'Oh – isn't Joyce there?'

'No,' Mrs Milray said. 'I don't think she felt too well. She left with Frances.'

'With Frankie?' Mark repeated. He opened the car door as far as he could with Mrs Milray in the way. 'I had better go and offer my apologies,' he said.

Mrs Milray nodded and stood aside. 'I think you better had,' she said, laughing a tinkling little laugh.

7

Frankie's hand gripped the receiver in an effort to keep her temper. 'Alan – what is going on?' she asked.

'How should I know? But if she is there, you tell her that I hadn't finished with her. You tell her that I'm here and I'm staying here until she comes back. She'll be back,' he said. 'She'll be back. Her son the artist is still here. Unless he's gone too. That'll be the day. That's what they want me to think. But you tell her I'm waiting.' He hung up.

Frankie held the phone, listening to the dialling tone. Her hand went out to the dial, then she drew it back, pressing it to her lips as she tried to work out what to do. She dialled Richard's number, not at all sure what she was going to say, but the phone just rang out. She switched the recorder back on and replaced the receiver.

There wasn't much she could do, except hope that Sylvia had the sense to stay wherever she was until Alan had cooled off a little. Frankie picked up her overnight bag and left, not at all sure that Richard would be as thankful to see her as she would be to see him. But she was going, all the same.

8

The sun hovered, dipping towards the quarry, an evening breeze lifting the leaves of David's sketch pad.

David picked up the pad and began to draw quickly, his pencil shading darker and darker the image of a fighting plane, black and menacing in a cloudless sky. The drawing was bringing his thoughts into focus, the nebulous thoughts of the quarry, Frankie, and the rape fields.

A turbulent past, a perilous future, a uniformly bland present; war, he supposed, as he blackened the war machine still further. And Frankie's direct, truthful eyes, as green as Ireland itself. Ireland? Perhaps. But war, anyway. Big wars, little wars, wars that strengthened what they sought to destroy. Courage and loyalty and truth. Because if truth was the first casualty, it was also the sole survivor, and that was why he wanted Frankie.

9

Frankie drove fast along the almost empty roads, accelerating still more as the grey buildings petered out behind her and the farming land took over from the factories and the warehouses. The street-lighting had begun to come on and Frankie obediently switched on unnecessary headlights, lighting the multi-coloured cat's eyes on the smooth new road, which stretched out ahead of her for what looked like forever. At last, it developed into the turn-off lane, and she was heading down the steep incline to the Caswells. She slowed the car down and negotiated the quarry bend with care. She frowned as she saw Alan's car, parked along the old quarry road, and slowed to a stop.

She switched off her engine and got out to look round the emptiness of Upper Caswell for a sign of life. She walked towards Alan's empty car, big and sleek and silent, and she called his name.

She could hear the fear and the anger, in her own voice.

'Alan?' she called again. 'Are you here?'

Chapter Four

1

Sylvia drove down the Caswells hill, sweeping round the quarry bend, only to jam on her brakes as she almost ran into the back of a parked car. As she realised that it was Frankie's car, she saw Frankie herself, running towards her from the old quarry road, where Alan's car was sitting. Sylvia pulled her own car on to the grass verge and scrambled out.

'What's the matter?' she asked, as Frankie ran up to her. 'What's happened?'

Frankie was staring at her. 'I could ask you the same question,' she said. 'Except that I know the answer.'

Sylvia sighed. 'No lectures, please, Frankie. I'm all right.'

Frankie took a deep breath and released it. 'I thought he'd – oh, I didn't know what to think. I thought he'd done something awful. His car was here, and not a sign of anyone. And he was drunk.'

'Drunk?' Sylvia rubbed her eyes, but it hurt, and she was much too tired to cope with Frankie's dramatics.

'He rang me,' Frankie said. 'He'd been drinking, so I guessed he'd had a row with you. And he was asking where you were, and then when I got back here I found his car like this in the middle of nowhere.'

'Oh, Frankie!' Sylvia snapped. 'Is that all? I thought something had really happened.'

'I didn't know what to think,' Frankie protested. 'He might have done anything.'

'Did you think he was burying me, or what?' Sylvia asked drily.

'I *told* you. I didn't know what to think. I was worried.'

Sylvia looked round. 'How long have you been here?'

Frankie shrugged. 'A couple of minutes, that's all.'

51

Sylvia shook her head. 'Really, Frankie. What did you imagine had happened? He's obviously left the car here for some reason and walked home.'

'Why?'

'I don't know, do I? Perhaps it broke down.'

'But what was he doing here? Why would he have gone out? He said he was waiting for you – he was making threats.'

Sylvia opened her car door. 'I think that he left the car here, walked home, and then got drunk and rang you. He wouldn't have driven after he'd been drinking, would he?' She got into the car and slammed the door, immediately relenting and winding down the window. 'Thank you for being worried about me,' she said. 'But I'm perfectly all right. He'll have cooled off by now.'

'He wasn't what I'd call cool twenty minutes ago,' Frankie said. 'Don't go back yet.'

Sylvia sighed extravagantly. 'I do live there, Frankie,' she said. 'I'm not going to feel barred from my own house.'

'What was it about this time?' Frankie asked, sitting on the bonnet of Sylvia's car.

'Nothing much,' Sylvia said. 'Now will you please get off the car, because I want to go home.'

But Frankie didn't move. 'Why do you put up with it?' she asked.

'I said no lectures. Please get off the car, Frankie.'

Frankie slid off the car with some reluctance, and Sylvia even got as far as starting the engine before seeing Richard. He was coming from the quarry, passing Alan's car. She felt that she couldn't really just drive off.

'Is something wrong?' he called as he approached.

Switching off the engine, Sylvia accepted the inevitable and got out of the car.

'Can't you see?' Frankie waved a hand in Sylvia's general direction.

'Richard knows,' Sylvia said impatiently.

Frankie looked from her to Richard. 'Oh?'

'He stopped him.'

'Good. I hope you hit him.' When Richard didn't answer, Frankie shrugged a little. 'I see you left your guests after all,' she said.

'No.' Richard leant against Frankie's car. 'The party's over, to coin a phrase. What's Alan's car doing there?' he asked. 'What's going on?'

'Frankie seemed to think that Alan was doing away with me,' Sylvia said.

'I just didn't understand why his car was here,' Frankie said hotly. 'I still don't.'

'Is Alan here?' Richard asked.

'No,' Frankie said. 'He's drunk, and waiting for Sylvia, because he's not finished with her, he says.'

'Oh, stop it!' Sylvia said. 'This is no big deal. He got drunk and rang Frankie, talking a lot of nonsense,' she explained to Richard. 'He got her worried, and now she doesn't think I should go home.'

Richard raised his eyebrows. 'I can't say I disagree with her,' he said, then frowned. 'But what's his car doing here?'

'We'll find out a lot quicker if I just go and ask him,' Sylvia said.'

'He can't have been here that long,' Richard said. 'The car was in your driveway not half an hour ago.'

Sylvia glanced at Frankie.

'But that's when he rang me,' Frankie said. 'He *did* drive it after that,' she said to Sylvia, with just a hint of triumph.

'Does that convey something?' Richard asked coldly.

Frankie ignored him.

'Alan never normally goes near a car if he's been drinking anything the least alcoholic,' Sylvia explained. 'He thinks it should be a hanging offence.'

Richard looked back over his shoulder at Alan's car. 'He wouldn't – ?' He stopped. 'This might sound silly, but I thought I heard someone in the wood. He wouldn't have tried getting back into my place that way, would he?'

Sylvia was shaking her head, but Frankie wasn't.

'He might, if he thought you were there,' she said to Sylvia.

'In that case, I suggest that we all leave him to get on with it,' Sylvia said sharply. 'I'm not there, and he'll be on his way back.'

Richard seemed unhappy. 'Perhaps I should go and have a

look,' he said. 'If he's drunk, he shouldn't really be driving about so close to the quarry.'

'Who says?' said Frankie.

'If that's all you can contribute – ' Richard began, and turned as they heard running feet.

'What's happened? What's wrong?' David came running up and stopped when he saw Sylvia.

'Nothing's wrong,' Sylvia said wearily.

'Where is he?' David demanded. 'What's his car doing there?'

Sylvia groaned. 'Not you too, please.'

Richard beckoned to David, wandering off a little way to explain the situation without further irritation to Sylvia, for which she was grateful. Sylvia sat down in the driving seat again. Literally, she thought with bleak humour, but by no means figuratively. Frankie's sense of drama was winning, and even David felt he ought to play some part, as he came over to her.

'I think he's right,' he said quietly. 'We should look for him. And I don't think you should go home until we know where he is.'

'Nothing's going to happen to me,' Sylvia said. 'It's over and done with.'

'That's not how it sounded when he rang me,' Frankie said. 'He was looking for you.'

'Come on, then.' Richard looked down the path. 'Perhaps we should take a torch,' he said. 'It's beginning to get a bit dark.'

'Alan keeps one in the car,' Frankie said, and all three set off down the quarry road. Sylvia watched as Frankie reached into the car and handed David the torch. Richard and David went off on their mission, and Frankie returned, leaning once again on Sylvia's car.

'Are you and Richard having a row, or what?' Sylvia asked.

Frankie shrugged. 'I wish I knew,' she said.

Headlights accentuated the gathering gloom as a car came up the hill from the village, round the bend in the road. Sylvia groaned as the car stopped, and Mark Rainford got out.

'Frankie? Isn't Joyce with you?' He crossed the road and Sylvia, at the wheel of her car, saw him glance at her, then look again, his eyes widening. 'What on earth's happened?' he asked.

Sylvia looked away.

'What's happened?' he asked again. 'Who did that?'

She turned back. 'You might as well tell him,' she said to Frankie.

'Alan,' Frankie said, quietly and reluctantly.

For the first time that Sylvia could remember, there was a reaction from Mark. His mouth opened slightly. 'Alan?' he repeated, looking to Sylvia for confirmation. 'Alan did that?'

Sylvia nodded, as philosophically as she could under the circumstances.

'Jesus,' Mark said, after a moment.

And that, Sylvia realised with relief, was as emotional as Mark was going to get. If he had had to turn up, at least he was an antidote to Frankie.

'Where is he now?' Mark asked, with a nod of his head at Alan's car.

'God knows,' Frankie said.

Mark looked round hopelessly. 'Do you think he's here somewhere?'

'David and Richard are having a look round,' Frankie said.

'Richard's here, is he? Does he know that his house looks like the *Marie Céleste*?'

'What do you mean?'

'I've just left there. It's standing open, and not a soul there. Fairy lights blinking on and off, food and drink all laid out and as silent as the grave. Very eerie.' He smiled. 'The clock chimed, and I nearly jumped out of my skin.'

'I suppose he knows,' Frankie said.

'I waited to see if he came back, but when he didn't, I decided to see if Joyce was with you. Mrs M said you'd taken her home.'

'Not literally,' Frankie said. 'I took her to her own home.'

'Well, she's not there now and I've forgotten my key.'

Frankie shrugged.

Sylvia saw David and Richard as they came back, running.

David got his breath back first. 'Does that phone work?' he asked, taking huge gulps of air.

She glanced at the old phone box, a relic of the days when Upper Caswell was a working quarry, but David was already bounding across the road. Richard was bent over, his hands on

55

his knees.

'What is it? What's wrong?' Frankie was asking.

Sylvia got out of the car, her face white. 'Richard? What's happened?'

'It's Alan,' he said, between gasps. 'There's been an accident.' He straightened up. 'We found him in the quarry,' he said. 'He must have fallen.'

Sylvia clutched at Frankie's arm. 'Come with me,' she said, beginning to run towards the road, but Richard stopped her.

'No – it's too dark now – it's dangerous. You don't know where he is.'

'Then show me!'

'I can't. I have to get my breath back.'

Frankie shot a look at him, and Sylvia saw the tiny shake of his head.

'What are you saying?' she asked. 'How bad is he?'

Richard went over to her. 'We went down,' he said. 'The opposite side isn't steep.' He looked helplessly at Frankie. 'I'm sorry,' he said to Sylvia.

Sylvia walked away from them, back to her car and stood on her own.

David came back. 'They said to wait here,' he told them. 'They'll get here as soon as they can.'

'Sylvia doesn't have to wait,' Richard said. 'Someone should take her home.'

'No,' she said.

All four looked at her.

'Will you show me where he is?' she asked David.

'It's too dark,' he said. 'I don't think there's anything you can do.'

2

Joyce stood in Richard's garden and shivered slightly. She had never seen anywhere that looked so obviously and suddenly deserted. Why was it, she wondered, that the idea of no-one being there was so frightening?

56

Her common sense rose to the surface with the thought. No-one there wasn't frightening. Someone there would be frightening. He was lucky he hadn't been burgled. She sat down on the terrace. Presumably he hadn't gone far, she thought. She'd wait, just to be on the safe side. As she waited, she could hear a clock inside chiming the quarter hours. It made the time pass slowly.

3

A police car, speeding dangerously down the hill towards them, slithered to a halt and a sergeant and a man in plain clothes got out. Frankie slid as far back into the shadows as she could.

'Sergeant Martin, Brampton,' the uniformed man said to Richard. 'There's been an accident reported?'

Richard told him briefly what they had found.

'Right, thank you. The ambulance is right behind.' He looked up the swiftly darkening quarry road. 'Can someone show us where he is?'

'Yes – I will.' David started towards the road.

'Can I come?' Sylvia almost made the sergeant jump. The two policemen turned.

'Dempster,' said the plain-clothes man. 'Detective Sergeant. What's happened to you, love?'

'She's been beaten up,' David said.

Sergeant Dempster walked towards him. 'And you are...?' he asked.

'David Newman.'

'Hang on, son. The ambulance is just coming.'

'And perhaps I could have your name?' Sergeant Dempster stepped towards Frankie. 'Oh – sorry! It's Frankie O'Brien, isn't it? I didn't recognise you.'

Frankie could cheerfully have stuck a knife in his ribs. As she tried to summon up some sort of answer, the ambulance came, pulling up beside them.

'Whereabouts?' one of the ambulancemen roared above the noise of the engine.

'I'll show you.' David jumped into the ambulance and it bumped its way over the verge on to the old road.

The policemen followed; Frankie stood for a moment on her own, then joined Richard. The blue flashing light on the police car made them look like a tableau. Mark standing by his car, Sylvia sitting half in, half out of hers. She and Richard leaning against her car, and no-one speaking.

For a little while, the only sounds were the far-off shouts of the police and ambulance crew and sporadic bursts of activity from the police car radio. There were so many things that she and Richard had to say to one another, and neither of them could begin.

She sneaked a quick look at Richard. Just a flick of her eyes in his direction, nothing more.

'What brought you back?' he asked, his voice low and almost surly.

It wasn't the way she had meant it to be and she didn't answer for a moment. When she did, it wasn't at all what she wanted to say.

'I changed my mind.'

Richard turned his head to look back at the quarry. 'You were just a bit too late,' he said. 'Weren't you?

Sergeant Martin returned with David, and they went to speak to Sylvia.

Frankie watched as Sylvia listened; she saw her shoulders droop and David's arm go round her. Mark joined her and Richard as Dempster returned.

'I gather that you already know,' he said quietly. 'Mr Blake is dead. I would like a word with everyone tonight if possible.'

'How would it be if we went to my house?' Richard asked. 'It's about three miles down the road. We can't all stand here all night.'

The sergeant looked relieved. 'Good idea,' he said. 'If someone could lead the way?'

'I will,' said Mark.

'I'll drive Sylvia,' Richard said. 'David – perhaps you could go with Frankie?'

Frankie opened her car door and looked across at David, who

detached himself from his mother.

'I could have driven her,' he complained mildly as he got into the car.

'Not with all the fuzz about, you couldn't.'

David closed the car door. 'They wouldn't have cared,' he said. 'This is like a private road. They wouldn't have done anything.'

Frankie started the engine and waited for Mark to turn his car. 'Don't you believe it,' she said grimly. 'Don't you believe it, David.'

4

David had tried to speak to Frankie once or twice on the drive to Hascombe's, but he hadn't known what to say. She wasn't speaking; she was just driving at the slightly funereal pace being set by Mark, her mouth in a thin straight line, her face drawn and tired.

He didn't know what to say, because he didn't know what he felt. He had felt nothing when he realised that Blake was dead. Certainly not grief. Not sadness, not pleasure, not anything at all. And he hadn't been prepared for his mother's reaction, when the police confirmed what everyone already knew. She had gone limp, just for a moment, before pulling herself together. And Frankie, tight-lipped and looking as though she was going to cry, puzzled him too.

It hadn't occurred to him that they would cry for Blake.

Frankie pulled up behind Mark in Hascombe's driveway, and everyone got out, with more door banging than seemed possible.

Joyce, dressed in very old clothes, suddenly appeared from the side of the house, and David was seized with a quite dreadful urge to laugh. It was like an old-fashioned farce with people popping up from everywhere.

'How long have you been here?' Mark asked.

Joyce looked puzzled as she saw the line of cars. 'I don't know,' she said abstractedly. 'About three quarters of an hour, I suppose. What's the matter?'

'There's been an accident,' Frankie said. 'It's Alan.'

'What's happened?' Joyce looked fearfully at Mark.

'He fell,' he said simply, 'at the quarry. I'm afraid he's dead, Joyce.'

'Dead?' Joyce stared at him. 'Alan?' She looked at Frankie. 'Alan's dead?'

'Let's get inside,' Hascombe said, pushing open the door and ushering Joyce down the hall to the sitting-room. Frankie followed behind him, with Mark. As Hascombe switched on the sitting-room lights, the night through the open French windows suddenly looked much blacker. Lights twinkled incongruously in the trees; Hascombe snapped off the switch and closed the windows.

'I didn't know what to do,' Joyce said. 'I mean, the place was deserted and these windows were open – I thought I'd better stay – you never know who might walk in and I didn't really know what else to do.'

'Very careless of me,' Richard said, finding chairs for the others. 'I just went off for a walk – I forgot that Mr and Mrs Rogers weren't here this evening.'

Frankie threw a questioning look at Hascombe, but he chose to ignore it. In fact, David thought, he had chosen to ignore Frankie all along.

Joyce had seen Sylvia now. 'What happened to you?' she asked, bewildered.

'Blake,' David said, feeling under an obligation to answer, since his mother wasn't.

'Why?' she asked. 'When?'

David shrugged. 'Don't ask me,' he said.

The policeman came in then, the one who had known Frankie. 'Mrs Blake?' he said.

'Sergeant Dempster, isn't it?' his mother said. 'I remember you.'

'If we could have a word somewhere in private?' he said.

Hascombe suggested the study and showed them the way. When he came back, Frankie spoke to him for the first time in David's hearing.

'When did that happen to Sylvia?' she asked.

'During the so-called party.'

'Here?' David said, surprised.

'When?' asked Frankie.

Hascombe looked from one to the other. 'You were talking to Joyce,' he said to Frankie. 'I came in for some more whisky, or God knows what would have happened.'

David sat down. '*Here*,' he said, almost to himself, trying to believe it.

'It had to happen, David,' Frankie said sharply. 'She couldn't keep it a secret for ever.'

David looked at her, wishing he could stop her and knowing that he couldn't.

'He's always observed protocol before,' Frankie explained to the others, her voice bitter. 'Other people's houses were definitely off-limits for wife-beating.'

'Don't, Frankie,' David said. 'You make it sound as though it happened every week.'

'Are you defending him?'

'No! I'm defending myself. If it had been a regular thing I could have done something. You couldn't tell when he'd do it.'

'What was he doing at the quarry?' Joyce asked.

David shook his head.

'Perhaps he went there to cool off,' Mark said.

He's cooled off all right now, David thought, with bleak satisfaction.

'But what happened?' Joyce asked. 'What made him fall?'

David took a sideways look at Frankie, wishing he hadn't shouted at her. Her eyes caught his for an instant, and he felt better.

'I suppose just because he was drunk,' said Mark. 'He wouldn't think what he was doing.'

Frankie was miles away, frowning slightly as she thought. David wondered what she felt. What she really felt. It was never too difficult to find out with Frankie, but he'd wait for a more suitable opportunity.

Richard went to the drinks cabinet. 'I don't know about anyone else,' he said.

'Why are the police bothering Sylvia?' asked Joyce. 'She should be in bed.'

'They like bothering people,' Frankie said. 'It's what they're good at.'

Richard took out glasses. 'They're only doing their job,' he said. 'There's been a fatal accident – they have to find out what happened.' He held up an empty glass. 'Joyce?'

'I could do with one,' Joyce said. 'Do you have brandy?'

'Brandy. Mark?'

'No thanks. To tell you the truth, I'd love a cup of tea.'

David wondered if a drink really helped. He didn't suppose he'd be asked, but he was. He accepted shyly, and was given a brandy.

'Medicinal,' Hascombe said, as he handed it to him. He gave Joyce hers and picked up his own whisky.

Frankie stood up. 'I'll get you some tea, Mark.'

'Oh – no, don't bother.'

'No bother.' She smiled a brittle smile at him. 'I'd like some coffee anyway.' She left the room, leaving the corridor door open, and Hascombe closed it firmly.

David sipped his brandy. The atmosphere between Hascombe and Frankie seemed quite unable to sustain life; he wondered just what had happened here tonight. He didn't suppose that his late stepfather would have been too far removed from the action.

5

Even making tea was a hassle in an unfamiliar kitchen. Especially to Frankie, to whom most domestic tasks were a hassle. A whisky bottle and two glasses sat on the table, looking somehow sordid in Mrs Rogers's gleaming, homely kitchen. Frankie removed them to the dresser and set about finding the constituent parts of a cup of tea. She found a tray and coffee mugs and, after a search, even found the tea, which had to be real tea, of course. Mrs Rogers would have no truck with teabags.

But finally she'd made it and she was negotiating the corridor with the tray to find that someone had shut the sitting-room door. The kick she gave it was perhaps a little more savage than was necessary.

Mark opened the door and took the tray from her, just as Sylvia and Sergeant Dempster came back in. The sergeant's words were rendered inaudible by the jet which screamed low overhead.

'Perhaps the sergeant would like some tea,' Richard said when the noise died down.

'Perhaps he would,' Frankie replied, sitting down.

'It's like living on the Heathrow flight path,' Mark said.

'Did you see that one earlier?' David asked. 'I felt as though I could reach up and touch it.'

'Oh yes,' said Joyce. 'I was in the garden. It made me *duck*. It's not right, you know. I'm sure they shouldn't fly so low where there are houses. And at this time of night! There are people with young children in these houses.'

'You were in the garden?' Mark said. 'But that's when I was trying to get in! What were you doing?'

'Digging,' Joyce said, slightly embarrassed. 'And that jet looked as though it was going to land on the lawn.'

'It's to do with flying under the radar,' Sergeant Dempster contributed, when he could get a word in.

'Well, they should do it somewhere else,' Joyce said.

Richard drained his glass. 'I was saying good night to a Mrs Milray,' he said with a smile. 'She was not at all amused. But they have to practise somewhere, I suppose.'

'Oh, for God's sake!' Frankie said. 'The police are only doing their job – the air force have got to practise somewhere!' She glared at him. 'Doesn't anything annoy you?'

'Oh yes,' he said readily. 'Some things annoy me, believe me.'

David stood up. 'Would you like me to make some more tea, Frankie?' he asked.

But his grand gesture was usurped by Mrs Rogers, who had knocked briskly on the door as he spoke. 'Mr Hascombe?' she said quietly. 'Is there something wrong?'

Chapter Five

1

Sylvia was being looked after by Mrs Rogers, and Sergeant Dempster had diplomatically refused tea made by anyone. Frankie sat down beside David. The sergeant had asked if anyone knew how the accident had happened, and they had all looked at one another and said no.

'You came from that direction, didn't you, son?' he asked David, who tried not to look too annoyed at being thus addressed.

'Yes,' he said. 'I'd been sketching.'

'Oh? Are you interested in drawing? My daughter's pretty good at that sort of thing.'

David tried to look politely interested.

'You'd been sketching at the quarry itself, had you?'

'Yes.'

Sergeant Dempster looked puzzled. 'And you didn't see your stepfather at all?'

'No.'

Frankie could feel waves of discomfort coming from David.

'But I wasn't there all the time,' he said. 'I came here – well, I meant to come here.' He looked at Frankie. 'I wanted to ask you something.'

'When would this have been?' Sergeant Dempster asked. 'Roughly?'

'I don't really know what time it was,' David said. 'It was still quite light. I came through the wood, but the party was still going on, and – and I didn't stay.'

'Why not?' Dempster asked.

'Well – I –' David looked at the floor. 'I wasn't going to come at all. I don't really like parties and things like that. I just wanted to see – to speak to Frankie. I thought it would be all right. But

64

then I heard the music and everything just –' He looked desperately at Frankie.

'It's not really any of your business, is it?' Frankie said to Dempster, her dislike of him growing. Why should David have to account for his shyness to this patronising person just because he was the police?

Dempster ignored her.

'So I just went back again,' David continued. 'I didn't want to have to look for Frankie with all the other people here.' He cleared his throat. 'When I got back, I saw Blake's car, and then everyone else. At first I thought there must have been a road accident. Anyway,' he concluded, 'that's when I ran along to see what was happening.'

'And you must just have missed Mr Blake,' the sergeant said.

'I must have.'

Richard looked up. 'I *thought* I heard someone,' he said. 'I must have been in the wood at the same time as David – I thought I heard someone, but I couldn't see anything.'

Dempster looked enquiringly at him. 'The wood?'

'I went for a walk,' he said. He glanced at David. 'We must have been just five hundred yards from the quarry when it happened,' he said. 'You must have left just before I arrived.'

'Ah well,' said the sergeant. 'If we could all arrange to be in the right place at the right time, accidents wouldn't happen at all, would they?'

It was rather as though this would be a Bad Thing, like the extinction of the tiger. Frankie groaned, audibly enough for Dempster to hear.

'And so you didn't see anything at the quarry, either, sir?'

'No,' Richard said. 'The accident must have happened by then, but I was just walking along the edge of the wood. I wasn't really near the quarry. Then I saw Blake's car. I walked down towards the road and found Mrs Blake and Frankie – I think they just happened to meet.' He glanced at Frankie for confirmation, but she didn't feel disposed towards supplying it. 'Anyway, they were wondering where Blake was, because his car was there – and when David turned up, he and I went to look.'

Frankie saw the sergeant's gaze move slowly round to her.

65

With ill-disguised displeasure, she explained about the phone call.

'When I saw his car, I was worried. Because he shouldn't have been driving,' she said. 'I was still there when Sylvia came, and she stopped to see what was going on. Then Richard and David went to look for him, and Mark arrived.'

Mark took the floor. 'I can't help at all, I'm afraid,' he said. 'I was in Westbridge all evening. When I got back, there was no-one at home and I thought Joyce must still be here. But I met Mrs Milray, and she said that it was all over.' He looked apologetically at Richard. 'I came in to say I was sorry I'd missed it,' he said. 'There was no-one here, so I waited, since I couldn't get in to my own house anyway.'

'And you didn't see Mr Blake at all?' Dempster asked.

'No. After about half an hour, I decided to see if Joyce was at Frankie's. And that's when I saw Frankie and Sylvia.' He shrugged. 'Not much help,' he said.

'And – Mrs Rainford, is it?' The sergeant turned to Joyce.

Frankie knew that he was just passing the time of day with her really – she was, after all, the only person who hadn't spoken to him. And Frankie knew what he was letting himself in for, but he didn't.

'Yes,' she said. 'That's right. I'm sorry, there's nothing I can tell you.' She proceeded to give the lie to her statement. 'I didn't know any of this was happening at all. To start with I was at home – well, I suppose to start with I was here, but Mark didn't turn up, and I really didn't want to stay all on my own, so I asked Frankie – Miss O'Brien – if she could take me home, and she did. I did some gardening, but Mark still didn't come, and I was beginning to get a bit worried, because he had said he'd be there, most particularly.' The last few words were accompanied by a baleful stare in Mark's direction.

'Well, thank you, Mrs Rainford, but I really just wondered if anyone knew how the acci –'

'Anyway, Frankie must think I'm a bit odd, coming back here like this, but what happened was that it occurred to me that Mark could have come directly here. I rang to see if he had but I thought that no-one could hear the phone. So I decided to walk back up. It was a lovely evening and I thought I might as well. The silly thing is, I forgot I was wearing my gardening clothes, so I was quite relieved that everyone had gone. But I –'

'It's quite all right, Mrs Rainford, I don't think we need trouble you.' It was said with an air of finality that even Joyce couldn't fail to notice. 'No-one can really throw any light on the accident,' he said. 'That's all I really wanted to know.'

And eventually, it was over. The police had gone, and with them the Rainfords, uttering the usual anything-I-can-do platitudes to David, who accepted them with an automatic good grace that Frankie was certain he didn't feel. Sylvia had been taken to her room by Mrs Rogers, and the moment was fast approaching when Frankie would be alone with Richard.

To delay it, perhaps, she turned as the front door closed and ran upstairs to see if Sylvia needed anything. This intelligence was thrown over her shoulder, not at Richard or David directly, but at either of them, both of them.

Mrs Rogers was just leaving the room when Frankie arrived. 'I'll bring you a hot drink,' she told Sylvia and left before the offer could be refused.

Sylvia sat heavily on the bed, her head in her hands.

'David's phoned the doctor,' Frankie said.

Sylvia looked up, dismayed. 'Why? I don't need a doctor.'

Frankie shrugged. 'The police asked him to,' she said. 'So he did.'

Sylvia closed her eyes. 'I'm not taking anything,' she said. 'I'm all right.'

'You don't have to take anything. Just let him have a look at you, at least.' Frankie sat on the chair beside the bed. 'What did they ask you?'

'About the row.' Her eyes opened slowly, painfully, to look at Frankie.

'Poking about in things that don't concern them, as usual,' said Frankie.

Sylvia shook her head slightly. 'To be fair, Sergeant Dempster said that it was probably none of their business. He was very polite – he was really quite kind.'

Frankie made a dismissive noise.

'They have to look into these things, 'Sylvia said. 'I told them that it had never happened before.' Her shoulders hunched slightly. 'But I don't suppose he believed me,' she finished.

Frankie's eyes filled with tears at the very idea of Sylvia, who had always gone to such lengths to conceal Alan's behaviour, having to tell Dempster, of all people. She reached out her hand and clasped Sylvia's. It was all over now.

'I said he'd been looking for me,' Sylvia continued. 'That he'd rung you. I said I thought he may have gone to the quarry thinking I was with David.' Her eyes searched Frankie's. 'Is that why he was there, Frankie?'

Frankie nodded slowly. 'Perhaps,' she said, standing up. 'I think you ought to get into bed now.'

'I don't have a nightie,' Sylvia said miserably. 'I'd better wait up for the doctor. I wish David hadn't rung him.'

'Well, he did. You can have my nightie,' Frankie said. 'I've got one in the car. I'll get it.'

2

David had been shown into a small back room.

'You needn't have bothered,' he said to Mrs Rogers. 'I could have slept on the sofa.'

'No bother,' she had said. 'You want to get some proper sleep.'

He heard feet pass the door as he stripped and lay down, and he stared at a small spider that crossed and recrossed the room along the top of the wall. Frankie was afraid of spiders; it always made him feel heroic when he could remove one for her. She used to babysit with him, when his mother and Blake were newly married, and the Blakes went to a lot of functions. He remembered the mixed feelings that he'd had the first time his mother had asked if he'd be all right on his own. It had meant that he was growing up, that he was entering Frankie's adult world. But it had meant that she wouldn't be there so often, to talk to him and make him laugh.

He couldn't really remember much about actually living with her; he remembered the house, of course, and had vague memories of Frankie's father, who was almost always in bed ill and around whom he had to be quiet. But Frankie had been a bright, star-like presence who came and went; he couldn't remember evenings spent with her. She always seemed to be going somewhere, always in a hurry. All he could really remember was a whiff of scent and a flash of green eyes. He'd gone off to school when he was eleven and he'd taken a photo of Frankie with him. He still had it.

3

Frankie reached into her car through the open window, to get her bag from the back seat. As she pulled it out, she saw David's sketch pad on the floor, almost disappearing under the passenger seat, and rescued it. The action reminded her of reaching into Alan's car for the torch. She had noticed then that the folder was gone from the passenger seat. Now, she realised something else, and she didn't know what it meant. She stood for a moment or two in the silky night air, wishing back a part of her life to live over again.

She closed the front door quietly and quickly ran upstairs before Richard saw her.

'It's in here somewhere,' she said to Sylvia, rummaging in the bag.

Sylvia had trusted her packing sufficiently to get undressed; Frankie produced the nightie with some relief and a flourish.

'I see Mrs Rogers kept her word,' Frankie said, as Sylvia got into bed. A mug of cocoa steamed on the bedside table.

Sylvia nodded. 'It's very good of her, but I don't really like cocoa at the best of times. And it must be eighty degrees outside.'

'Still, you should drink it,' Frankie said. 'It'll help you sleep.'

Frankie popped the sketch book into her bag, and picked it up.

'Frankie?' Sylvia's voice sounded strange.

'Yes?' Frankie turned.

'What were you doing at the quarry?'

Frankie put down the bag. 'I told you,' she said, puzzled.

Sylvia looked unconvinced, and Frankie's eyes widened.

'Are you saying you don't believe me?' she asked.

'I don't know,' Sylvia said.

A knock at the door prevented Frankie's response.

'The doctor's here, Mrs Blake,' Mrs Rogers said.

Frankie went out as the doctor came in and waited on the landing. After a few moments, he emerged.

'Nothing that nature won't take care of,' he said, closing the door. 'And I don't think she'll have any trouble sleeping tonight. But,' he said, producing a prescription, 'I've written this just in case she could do with something over the next few days.' He handed Frankie the piece of paper. 'Just let her do whatever she feels like doing.' He glared at her. 'And that includes crying, if that's how she feels. It's perfectly natural, you know.'

Frankie showed him to the door, and could think of no other way to postpone the moment that made her heart sink. She walked slowly along the hall and took a deep breath before opening the sitting-room door.

Richard sat by the screened-off fireplace. 'How's Sylvia?' he asked.

'She's all right,' Frankie said, closing the door. 'The doctor says to leave her alone, more or less.'

He nodded briefly.

'I want to know what you meant,' she said. 'When you said I'd changed my mind too late.'

'Oh, that. Nothing. Nothing at all.' He finished his drink and rose.

'You meant that it was my fault that Alan fell. Didn't you?'

His back was to her as he poured himself another drink. 'I didn't mean anything,' he said, turning round. 'It was just said in the heat of the moment.'

'The heat of the moment! You couldn't have timed it better if you'd rehearsed it!'

He replaced the stopper. 'I can assure you I didn't,' he said.

'Then you meant it.'

'It was a stupid thing to say and it wasn't true. I was angry, that's all. Can't we just forget it?'

'Oh sure – forget it. You're laying all this on me and then you say forget it. Why was it my fault?'

'It *wasn't* your fault.' He sat down, and rubbed his eyes. 'It's late, and we're both tired. Can't it at least wait until morning?'

'No. Sylvia will be here in the morning. I want to know now. If

I'd stayed – what were you going to do? Would it have stopped Alan going to the quarry?' She poured herself a brandy.

He didn't answer, and she had to know. She put down the bottle. 'Would it?' she asked again, walking over to him.

'How should I know?' he asked. 'You didn't stay, did you?'

'I couldn't,' Frankie said. 'How was I supposed to know? You didn't tell me about Sylvia!'

Richard sipped his drink and waited for a moment before he spoke. 'Why did you go?' he asked. 'Are you still saying it had nothing to do with Blake?'

'I never did say that,' she said. 'I said I had to think. I was confused.'

'But not for long? You were at the quarry when Sylvia got there – what made you come back? Did you sort yourself out?'

Frankie banged her brandy glass down on the table. 'I think I've had enough interrogation for one night,' she said, walking towards the door.

'That's right,' he said. 'Run away again.'

'I came back to be with you,' she said angrily. 'God knows why!'

4

Sylvia lay awake, listening to the muffled sounds reaching her from downstairs. She couldn't hear the words, just the rise and fall of the voices – Frankie's, angry and imperative, Richard's conciliatory and quiet, as they finally got the chance to have their row. About what? Alan? Her?

She had drunk the cocoa, despite the inordinate heat, and it was helping her to sleep. Now it all seemed like a dream, like something that was happening to someone else. Was it wrong, she wondered, to want to sleep? The numbness had started long before they found Alan. It had started when Richard had walked into his kitchen and found them.

It had sustained her through the rest of the evening, had protected her during the interview with Dempster; it had allowed her to talk to Frankie, without letting herself fall under the green-eyed spell that she could cast on everyone.

71

And now, as the voices died away, it was allowing her to sleep. Whatever the row was about, she thought, Frankie would have won. It would be Richard who was doing any apologising that had to be done, making any concessions that had to be made. Not Frankie. Never Frankie.

<h1 style="text-align:center">5</h1>

Frankie walked over to the tape recorder, removing the full tape and putting it away in its box. It gave the machine an odd, one-eyed look, Richard thought. She unplugged it and pulled out the speaker connections.

'Why wouldn't you stay?' he asked, trying to make the question sound as conversational and uncontentious as possible.

She abandoned the tape recorder and picked up her brandy, giving a small, preparatory sigh.

'Why do you want me?' she asked, with the candour which he knew would always take him by surprise.

'That's an odd question,' he said. It was an even odder answer, but he thought it wiser not to remark on that.

'What do you want me *for*?' she tried, as though altering the form of the question would bring it down to his level of comprehension. She frowned when he smiled. 'I'm serious,' she said.

'I can see that.'

'Well?'

'I honestly don't understand the question.'

'All right.' She sat on the floor, her legs curled under her. 'Am I a passing fancy, that will have run its course in a week or two? Do you think that's what you are? Or are you, for instance, intending marrying some respectable widow and keeping me on as your mistress?'

He was still trying to come to terms with this unlikely image of Frankie when she continued.

'Or do you see me as a wife? Do you just want things to go on as they are right now, or what?'

He looked at her, curled up like a cat on the rug and covered his mouth in a gesture of deep thought to mask the involuntary smile. When he felt sufficiently recovered, he leant forward. 'Are you seriously suggesting that I have any say in the matter?' he asked. 'You'll be whatever you want to be and you know it. And I'll either accept it or I won't. That's the choice I'll get – not this wonderful array of possibilities.'

'Never mind that. You must know what you want.'

'Who must? But as it happens, I believe that I want you to marry me.'

Her face fell at the suggestion, which wasn't entirely encouraging, but since he held out no hope at all, it wasn't too much of a blow.

'But I'd be a terrible wife,' she said. 'I can't cook, and I can't sew, I can't run a house. The only thing I can do you're getting already for free.' She smiled.

'That might worry me if I were a male chauvinist pig of limited means,' he said. 'But I'm not. Can I ask – has this got any vague connection with my original question?'

She nodded. 'I was talking to Mrs Milray,' she said.

Richard frowned. 'At the party?' he asked. 'First to arrive and last to leave? She knows you, doesn't she?'

'She knows you, too,' Frankie said.

'She does now,' he agreed.

'Mrs Milray said that you should have been on the Birthday Honours List,' she said.

Richard's eyebrows rose. 'Who did she train with?' he asked. 'The KGB?'

'Why weren't you?'

'Didn't Mrs Milray tell you?'

Frankie uncurled her legs and stood up to retrieve her untouched brandy. 'She hinted,' she said. 'She thought it might be the company you keep. Like me.'

'What?' He took out a cigar and Frankie handed him the matches. 'Come off it, Frankie! What does she know about it?'

Frankie sipped her brandy. 'She knows me a lot better than you do,' she said. 'And she could be right.'

The match flared and Richard inhaled the strong smoke. 'She isn't,' he said.

'I don't want to stop you getting a knighthood or whatever.' She sat on the floor again.

He extinguished the match with a stream of smoke. 'What makes you think I want one?' he asked.

'Don't you?' Frankie looked startled.

'They write to you, asking how you feel. I told them – politely – that I think the whole thing is a ridiculous waste of time.'

She frowned, obviously unsure of whether or not to believe him. 'When?' she asked, suspiciously.

'At least a month before I ever met you. I can prove it, if you like,' he added with a wave of his hand towards the bureau. 'The letter's in there, somewhere.'

She shook her head.

'And it wasn't anything as elevated as a knighthood,' he said. 'That wasn't why you left, surely?'

'Not just because of that,' she said. 'She told me about Amanda.'

Richard frowned. 'Amanda?' he asked. 'Oh! *Mandy* – sorry, I didn't recognise her Sunday name.' He nodded. 'I should have told you. How does this Mrs Milray know so much?'

Frankie shrugged. 'Why didn't you tell me?' she asked.

Richard pushed ash around the ashtray with his cigar. 'The moment never seemed right,' he said.

Frankie's eyes widened. 'Do we need right moments?' she asked.

'No,' he said. 'Probably not.' He absent-mindedly doodled in the ash, drawing a swastika for some reason. Probably deeply Freudian. A memory that Frankie didn't have. At least he had been too young to fight. 'Perhaps I should say that the moment had passed,' he said. 'It began to assume an importance that it doesn't really have.'

Frankie still didn't understand. She looked at him earnestly. 'I'd have thought it would have come up quite naturally,' she said. 'She's the same age as me, isn't she?'

'Just about.'

'Well then. What was so difficult about saying that you had a daughter my age?'

Richard smiled. 'It leaves a little to be desired as opening

74

gambits go,' he said. 'When I met you, I really didn't want to draw your attention to the age difference.'

'I need the age difference,' she said.

Richard rubbed out the swastika. 'You didn't leave just because of that, either,' he said.

She stood up. 'It didn't help,' she said.

'*Did* Blake have something to do with it?'

'Something,' she admitted. 'But maybe we do need right moments. This isn't one.'

She sat down on the sofa suddenly, as though she had run out of strength, and he realised that he had completely overlooked the effect that Blake's death would have had on Frankie. Whatever their relationship, it had been a long one.

'I'm sorry,' he said. 'I hardly knew him. It must be hard for you.'

Her eyes were far away though they looked at him. 'I'd almost forgotten,' she said. 'That's horrible, isn't it? It's as though it hadn't really happened. I just feel as though he'll still be around tomorrow.' She put down the drink. 'I don't really want this,' she said. 'I think I'll just go to bed.'

'I won't be long,' he said. 'I'll just finish this.' He lifted the cigar as he spoke and ash fell on to his shirt in a dismal, dispirited fashion. Who the hell was Mrs Milray?

6

Frankie thankfully removed her clothes and was looking in her overnight bag for her nightie for some minutes before remembering that she had given it to Sylvia. David's sketch pad came to the surface again and she picked it up.

She lay on the bed, turning the pages, smiling at the detailed little drawings. They were all of the quarry with only the shadows changing as she flicked through. All except one; that was of a plane, black against the sky, casting an enormous shadow on a very small town. It wasn't really a sketch, not a faithful reproduction of what David was looking at, like the others. It was almost a cartoon, of the jet he'd said he felt that he could reach up and touch.

She closed the book and pulled the sheet over her, though even it felt heavy in the hot, still night. Leaving the light on for Richard, she closed her eyes, but the image of the cartoon plane danced in her tired mind, black and menacing, overshadowing everything. It must have been that plane that she'd heard when Alan rang her up. Swooping over Alan's house, like some monstrous bird of ill-omen.

But no, that was wrong. It couldn't have been the same plane, because Mrs Milray was the last to leave.

Somehow, that certainty seemed to make everything all right, and Frankie's racing thoughts slowed to a temporary, sleep-induced halt.

Chapter Six

1

Richard was in the little breakfast-room off the kitchen, addressing himself with a marked lack of enthusiasm to a boiled egg.

'There's no law says you *have* to eat breakfast,' Frankie said.

He looked up. 'You shouldn't try to work on an empty stomach,' he said.

Frankie thought for a moment that he meant his book. It seemed a little callous, with Sylvia and David in the house, even if he hadn't known Alan all that well. 'Were you thinking of working?' she asked.

'Sylvia spoke to me last night. She's worried about the factory.' He took a spoonful of egg. 'I think she's just fastened on to it as something else to think about, but I said I'd help you out as best I could until something gets sorted out.'

Frankie went through to the kitchen, pleased to find it empty, and started making coffee. She propped open the door. 'It's Sunday, Richard,' she reminded him. 'They've stopped Sunday work at the factory.'

'I know.'

She came back through. 'Would you like coffee?'

'No thanks. I've got tea here.' He poured himself a cup as he spoke. 'But I don't want to feel like the new girl at St Trinian's, so I thought I'd go in today and see what's what.' He folded the paper to the next page without the struggle that other people have. He didn't drop the Business Section in the marmalade like the rest of mankind. Frankie could never be sure whether she trusted this aspect of Richard. 'I thought you might come with me,' he said. 'Show me the ropes?'

'Yes, sure. But I'll have to be here when Sylvia comes down.'

'Of course. I think I'll go in and see you when I see you. If you can't get away, it doesn't matter.'

Mrs Rogers appeared, tutting about the inadequacy of Richard's breakfast, apologising for having failed to foresee the early start being made for a Sunday and shaking her head over Frankie's refusal to eat anything at all.

2

Sylvia awoke to daylight, momentarily unaware of her circumstances; for the foreign bed, the wallpaper, the source of light puzzled her for a second or two. When she remembered it took her sleep-numbed brain a moment to react. When reaction did set in, she cried. She heard the gentle tap on the door, but she didn't acknowledge it. She had to get the tears out of her system. She had to face people in her own time.

She had watched Frankie last night, so obviously happy to be Richard Hascombe's hostess, despite the awfulness of the evening. Her mind flinched from the scene that followed and her embarrassment at being rescued by Richard Hascombe.

But then they had talked, and the embarrassment had gone, to be replaced by the numbness. In that numbness, she had spoken to Richard about Frankie in a way that she could never normally have contemplated.

She had asked him point blank if he knew what he was taking on, but he had just smiled, and she could say no more than that he would answer to her if Frankie got hurt. But she had said it, and he'd listened.

And then he'd left to go back to his guests, and she had heard Frankie's voice. She had no desire to eavesdrop again, and she had left. She felt again the bleak, angry determination that had enveloped her as she slipped away from the party. And now Alan was dead.

She had to get herself together. There was all the official, bureaucratic side of sudden death to be dealt with. Identification, picking up belongings, post-mortems, death certificates, inquests, funerals. She had coped with death before, from the other side of the counter, in her insurance days. And she had coped with Joseph O'Brien's death and Frankie's grief-stricken conviction that she had hastened his end.

She wondered how Frankie was feeling. And what she had been doing at the quarry. She tried to push away the thought that had lodged itself in her mind. It was absurd. It was nonsense. But it was there.

3

David tiptoed away from his mother's room and met Frankie at the top of the stairs. 'She's still asleep,' he said.

'Good. That'll make her feel better,' Frankie said briskly. 'I found this in the car,' she said, handing him his sketch pad. 'Come and have some breakfast.'

David was surprised to find that he was very hungry. He supposed he shouldn't really be, but his stomach insisted on rumbling in a totally insensitive fashion. Mrs Rogers fussed round him, which he enjoyed. Frankie seemed a little far away from him. He supposed gloomily that everyone had liked his stepfather better than he had.

He had been shocked when he realised that he was dead, but only in the same detached way that he would have been if it had been a stranger. He hadn't thought of the effect it would have on his mother, or Frankie, or anyone. There had been a sort of closing-down, a shutting-off, that had pushed the consequences from his mind. He couldn't feel sorry; he could only feel relieved.

Frankie held a piece of toast in her hand, which she wasn't even thinking of eating. Her eyes were fixed on some point beyond the breakfast-room window, but she wasn't actually looking at anything. Her face was serious and a little pale.

'Doesn't Mr Hascombe eat breakfast?' David asked, because he didn't like the silence.

'Sorry?' She brought her mind back from wherever it had been and looked at him, her eyes blank. 'Oh – yes. He's had his already. He's gone into the office, so that he knows what's what

79

for tomorrow.'

David finished his bacon and eggs, reflecting on the fickleness of society, which accepted Hascombe and Frankie as a couple, even if it didn't entirely approve, and which didn't even consider him and Frankie. Ten years' difference as opposed to twenty-six.

His mother appeared in the door, dressed and reasonably well-looking, if you ignored the bruises.

'Good morning,' she said, and her voice was hoarse.

Frankie picked up the coffee-pot. 'Freshly made,' she said. 'Or would you rather have tea?'

'Coffee will be fine.' Sylvia sat down as Frankie poured the coffee and looked across at David. 'Are you all right?' she asked.

'Yes, of course,' he said. 'How do you feel?'

'Better,' she said. 'I'll be all right.' She turned to Frankie. 'Did I hear you say Richard has gone into the office?' she asked as she took her cup.

Frankie nodded.

'I don't feel very much like driving – would you take me in? I think I'd like to see what it's all about.'

'Yes, of course, if you want to.' Frankie looked surprised. 'Are you sure you feel up to it?'

'I think so. I'll have to go home and change first, though.'

Sylvia smiled carefully, which was all she could do, David thought angrily, with a cut lip.

4

Frankie drove the short distance to the Blakes' house and waited in the car until Sylvia was ready.

The sun was climbing high again as they set off and the deserted Sunday road looked bright and efficient, its newly-painted white lines gleaming.

Not much was said on the way; Frankie tried the occasional remark, but Sylvia uttered only monosyllables in reply. She drove into Market Brampton, where she stopped and started at the traffic lights which punctuated the main street. It was a wide road, a market town road where stalls and sideshows had once livened up the town on market days. Usually cars were parked in slanted rows down each side of the street, with anxious drivers waiting for the moment when they could pull out. Today the wide road was empty. The road forked into a Y at the top. The building that separated the two arms had once been the seventeenth-century corn-hall, but the Victorians had taken care of that. Frankie took the left fork, the one which led into the by-ways and cobbled alleys and the old warehouse which was now Blake's Electronic Components Ltd.

The car bumped and jolted over the gravel-strewn area that served as a car park. When she stopped, Frankie turned to speak to Sylvia, but Sylvia was miles away from the Blake car park; Frankie doubted that she knew she was there. It was difficult to know how to deal with the situation, because everything Frankie thought of saying she rejected as unsuitable. None of the stock phrases applied. Alan and Sylvia had kept up appearances, but even the image of their marriage had been shattered last night and the Time is a Great Healer encouragement normally given to the bereaved seemed singularly out of place.

'Do you still want to come in?' she asked.

'Yes.' But Sylvia leant back in the seat. 'Not yet though.'

Frankie made to open the door.

'No, stay. I want to talk.'

It was a command; Frankie obeyed.

'I don't know how you really felt about Alan,' Sylvia said suddenly.

'Neither do I,' Frankie replied. 'I can't pretend I liked him – not after everything I've said about him. But I will miss him.'

'I know,' Sylvia said. 'We didn't have much of a marriage – not in the conventional sense, anyway. And you think that I put up with his behaviour because I was – what? Afraid to do anything else?'

Frankie shook her head. 'No, not afraid. I never thought you were afraid. Too stubborn to do anything else, maybe.' There was no maybe about it, but she was trying to be polite. Sylvia's sheer, awe-inspiring obstinacy in remaining married to Alan was quite remarkable.

'It was beginning to fall apart,' Sylvia said. 'Even before last night. But we knew that the disintegration was inevitable, like buying a car. Before that, we understood one another. We had a bargain and it worked. It worked for us.' She paused.

Frankie didn't try to speak. She was obviously being asked just to listen.

'David's glad he's dead, isn't he?' Sylvia said.

'No.' Frankie answered. 'No, I don't think he is. If you want the truth, I don't think he feels anything much about it at all, except that Alan won't be around any more, which doesn't upset him.'

'I always want the truth,' Sylvia said. 'That's why the marriage worked as long as it did. And it did work. Because we knew the truth about one another right from the start. And that was no-one else's business until last night. Not even yours.'

Frankie nodded.

'I understood him, you see,' Sylvia said. 'David never did, but that's hardly surprising. I don't know if you really understood him. He thought you did.'

Frankie was a little surprised to hear it, but she supposed they had worked together amicably enough. It had been, she imagined, a bit like his marriage. 'It's you I find difficult to understand,' she said.

'I know. But it was a bargain. He gave me a nice house and I gave him a nice home.' She smiled quickly, not so much a smile as a slight spasm of face muscles. 'That's over-simplifying, but that was what it was in essence. We accepted one another – that's a kind of love, in its way.'

Frankie's eyebrows rose. 'And you accepted being treated like that?' She nodded towards Sylvia herself, at the bruises.

'No. That's why it was beginning to disintegrate. And even if it could have survived that, last night he brought other people into it. That's what I couldn't accept.'

'But it was all right as long as no-one else *knew*?' Frankie's voice almost squeaked with incredulity.

'In a way.'

Frankie shook her head. 'What for?' she asked. 'What was it all for?'

'You know what it was for.'

82

'So that you can live in a house like that? Send David off to school – so that you can buy good clothes and drive a sports-car? It was that important to you?'

Sylvia ran a hand through her hair. 'Yes, it was,' she said. 'I could have begun to regard his violence as an occupational hazard. I even understood it, in a way.'

'Oh?'

'Alan liked to feel that he was in command of everything. And usually money, or position, lets you be in command. But there are situations where money and position don't count – that's when Alan would hit out. When it was the only way he could prove he was stronger.'

Frankie had had enough of being polite. 'I'm surprised that you couldn't make room for what he did last night,' she said. 'I'm sure there must have been some good reason.'

'I think I could have done. Oh, I drove round, working out how I was going to leave, and when, and where I would go. But I had more or less decided against it. Even though he'd broken the rules. So – you're right. I would have just taken it on board too. Are you very shocked?' She opened the door.

'No,' Frankie said, though it would have been truer to say yes. But perhaps, she thought, shocked was the wrong word. She was baffled. Living by rules was so alien to her that she couldn't begin to understand.

5

Richard was surprised to see Sylvia and pleased to see Frankie.

She smiled when she came in and he smiled back. She didn't seem twenty-six years younger than him, he thought. Sometimes, she seemed older, much older, than he would ever be. There was something ageless about Frankie.

'I hope you don't think this too unseemly,' Sylvia said, as she sat down. 'But I'd like to understand what's what from today.'

'I think it's very sensible,' he said. 'As long as you feel up to it.'

'Oh, I'm all right.'

'You won't like this,' he said. 'I've not so much come in to sort out the situation as to confirm it.'

'We're in trouble?' Sylvia asked, unsurprised.

'Did Alan talk to you about the business?'

'Not exactly. But I knew he was worried.'

Richard pushed some papers towards her. 'Do you understand balance sheets?' he asked.

'No. I'm ashamed to say I don't.' She relaxed a little. 'Just tell me.'

'Well,' Richard began. 'There are orders, which might seem to you to be all that we need. But we can't fulfil them without some expansion, and we can't expand without credit. We're still paying the interest on the last loan, and the bank won't extend any more credit. In fact, it may call in its current loan.'

He pulled the papers back to his side of the desk. 'Alan wanted a very large injection of cash, and he thought that my bank would provide it for a slice of the eventual profits. But I advised them that I didn't consider it a good investment. So,' he concluded, 'I am the author of your financial misfortune, I'm afraid.'

Sylvia thought for a moment. 'But yesterday – you told me you were prepared to invest.'

'Personally. I was prepared to try to work out a survival plan, and use my own money. I still am, if you want me to.' He smiled seriously. 'It could all end in tears. And it could bring us up against the union.' He stood up. 'The choice is simple. Bring in the Receiver and cut your losses, or try to fight and run the risk of losing the lot.' He took out his cigars and lit one.

'What would be the alternative to losing the lot?' she asked.

Richard was surprised; he had thought she was going through the motions of taking an interest.

'A streamlined, healthy business,' he said. 'Smaller, more cost-effective – all hands to the pump, that sort of thing. It can be quite exciting.' He tried unsuccessfully to blow a smoke ring. 'And it gives you ulcers,' he added.

Sylvia looked thoughtful. 'Then that's what we'll do,' she said, after a moment.

Richard smiled. He would have thought that Sylvia would always prefer to cut her losses.

'Good,' he said. 'But in the meantime, there are more

84

immediate problems.' He waved a hand over the paper-strewn desk. 'As you can see.'

They spent the morning sorting out what Blake might have meant by this, and what he'd done with that. He had obviously been in the day before; he'd opened the Saturday mail, and written the odd cryptic comment on some of it. Only Frankie really knew what she was doing and Richard began to wonder why he'd bothered to come in. All he was doing was producing problems for Frankie to solve.

'There are two letters here about the ZR39/1T, whatever that is,' he said.

'Oh yes – I'll deal with them. It's a little –'

'No, thank you!' Richard said. 'I'll survive without knowing for the moment. And there's a letter from the bank,' he said grimly. 'I'd better deal with that.'

Frankie took a small pile of stuff into her own office.

'A red reminder from the Electricity Board, ditto re the telephones,' said Sylvia.

'A letter saying that this firm's buyer is coming tomorrow to discuss the non-delivery of twelve gross of ZR39/1T,' Richard said.

His eyes met Sylvia's. 'Are you sure you want to go through with this?' he asked.

'Oh, yes,' she said. 'I'm quite sure.'

6

The knock on the outer office door startled Frankie; she had barely recovered her composure when Sergeant Dempster walked in to shatter it again.

'What are you doing here?' she asked curtly.

Sergeant Dempster closed the door quietly. 'The young man said I'd find you here.'

He sat down uninvited and mopped his brow with a paper handkerchief. His sandy hair was receding now, Frankie noticed. He reached into his inside pocket and drew out a piece of paper. 'It seems Mr Blake left you a note,' he said, holding it out to her.

Frankie stared at him. 'Left me a note? What do you mean, *left* me a note? That makes it sound as if he killed himself.'

The merest nod confirmed her statement. 'Photocopy,' he said. 'The original's with the coroner.'

Frankie took it, and read.

> *Frankie. This is a dreadful mess. I hope you can understand –*
> *I couldn't face starting all over again. I know I'm running out*
> *on you, but I'm a coward, and you're not. You'll get on better*
> *without me. You'll cope – you always do.*
>   *Alan*

She re-read it, but it still made no sense. It was his writing, hasty and untidy. She looked at Dempster, bewildered.

'It'll be up to the inquest, of course,' he said. 'But it does seem fairly cut and dried.'

'Not to me,' Frankie said.

Sergeant Dempster's fair lashes closed in exaggerated disbelief. 'You're saying that it's *not* a suicide note?' he said.

Frankie glanced at it again. 'I don't know what it is,' she said. 'It doesn't make sense.'

Dempster leant his elbows heavily on the desk. 'Frankie,' he said, tapping his chest. 'It's me you're talking to. It makes sense to me. As far as we can gather, his business was on its last legs, for a start. And judging by the state of his wife last night, his marriage didn't have too long to go. And then we found this note – it had all got too much for him.'

'Not for Alan,' Frankie said hotly. 'He'd let a wife and a business slip through his hands before – he just went out and bought himself new ones.'

'But he didn't have you to reckon with then, did he?' Dempster said.

Frankie could feel her face growing hot. 'I don't think you have any right to speak to me like that,' she said.

'I don't think anyone can hear me,' he replied.

Frankie rose, the note in her hand. 'Mrs Blake's in the office next door,' she said. 'Let's see what she has to make of it.'

A frown appeared momentarily on the sergeant's brow. 'You're going to show that to his wife?'

'Yes.' Frankie stood up. 'She'll hear about it anyway, if you're insisting it's a suicide note.'

'But you are going to ask her if *she* knows what it means?'

'Yes. Because I don't.'

She walked towards the door, but the sergeant's hand lightly caught her arm. 'Let me get this straight,' he said. 'You are saying that you aren't satisfied that this is a suicide note?'

'I don't know what it is. Why would he write *me* a suicide note?'

The sergeant looked at her in frank disbelief. 'Oh,' he said with a reluctant little laugh, 'you're a cool one, all right.'

Frankie had been called a number of things by a number of people. Cool wasn't one of them. She knocked and went in, explained briefly the sergeant's presence and handed the note to Sylvia. 'Read it,' she said, and her hand shook as she held it out.

She watched as Sylvia's eyes scanned the lines and waited for her reaction. She looked up at Frankie and said nothing for a long moment.

'What does it mean?' she said, when at last she spoke.

'I haven't the faintest idea,' Frankie said.

Sylvia handed the note back without further comment, and Frankie tossed it down in front of Richard.

He read it, folded it and held it out to her. 'It seems clear enough to me,' he said.

'Well,' Dempster said, relieved to have someone on his side at last. 'We're reasonably satisfied that Mr Blake took his own life. But obviously, the inquest will rule on that.'

Sylvia's head shot up. 'Suicide?' she said. 'But that's nonsense.'

Frankie turned to Dempster, a hint of triumph in her eyes.

'What other construction would you put on it, Mrs Blake?' he asked gently.

'I don't know. It wasn't addressed to me.' Sylvia looked pointedly at Frankie. 'But Alan didn't kill himself, I'm sure of that. It was an accident, that's all.'

'Like I say, that what the inquest's for. You'll be able to put whatever points you like to the coroner – it might be an idea to speak to your solicitor, though,' he added. 'Or to this one.' His head jerked in Frankie's direction, and she pushed past him into her own office.

She still had the note in her hand and she read it again. After some moments, the sergeant came back through and left without a word. As soon as the door closed, Sylvia followed him through.

'What does it mean, Frankie?' she asked.

Frankie spread it out on the desk in front of her. 'I don't know,' she said.

Sylvia leant over. 'It's written to you,' she pointed out.

'I know that,' Frankie said. 'And I know what Dempster thinks. Is that what you think too?'

'Dempster thinks he killed himself,' Sylvia said. 'I don't.' She straightened up. 'He says he's running out on you,' she said. 'What does he mean?'

'I don't know,' Frankie said, folding the note carefully.

Richard came in, papers in his hand. 'Frankie – could you make a note to telephone the Electricity Board and the Post Office first thing tomorrow morning? Tell them I'll be settling the accounts – not the firm. Me, personally. And this man –'

Frankie stared at him. 'Are you serious?'

Richard didn't answer the question. 'This man,' he said, throwing the letter on to her desk. 'Can you try to put him off? I don't have the slightest idea why his order hasn't been delivered.'

'Is that all you're going to say?'

'It's a letter from some people who – '

'Not that!'

Richard sat down as Sylvia went back into the other office. 'But that's what I'm talking about,' he said.

'Why?'

'Because, unlike Blake, I don't hit women,' he said. 'But that's what I want to do, Frankie, and if I talk about anything but work, that's probably what I will do.'

'Why?' Frankie asked again.

'I won't be lied to.'

Frankie's face burned with indignation. 'You haven't been lied to,' she said.

'I don't want to discuss it.'

She picked up the letter he'd brought in. 'Fine,' she said. 'In that case, you can discuss this. You can cancel this visit if you like, but there will be others. Irate customers weren't Alan's cup of tea. He'll have found himself an office equipment exhibition to go to tomorrow, and I've no doubt whatever that you'll find a memo on his desk telling me exactly what lies to tell this man when he comes. Because that's what's Alan Blake was, Richard. A liar. He will have lied to you to try to get your backing – he will have lied to this firm about the completion of their order. And that's what this is,' she said, picking up the note and unfolding it. 'It's lies.'

'Lies?' Richard jumped to his feet. 'Why in God's name would he write you a pack of lies?'

'I don't know!' It was like some monstrous practical joke; she swivelled her chair to look out of the window at the old buildings which surrounded Blake's, their roofs sagging slightly, their lines merging into one another. Now and then a new, tall, flat-roofed building broke up the almost fluid view, like lighthouses in a heaving sea. Market Brampton had only recently developed a conscience about its heritage; the confused mixture of architectural values might offend a more artistic eye, but it soothed Frankie's.

'I told you yesterday morning that it was none of my business,' he said. 'It still isn't – don't you understand? Why tell lies about it?'

The side roads were quiet, but despite that a traffic warden prowled around, keeping her eye on a brown Avenger. Surely they were out of season on a Sunday? She was cheated of her quarry as the driver sprinted back to the car.

'Are you listening to me?'

Ah, a lorry was unloading across the road. Some sort of special delivery. The young man who heaved the packing cases was shirtless and brick-red with the sun.

'Frankie!'

She turned slowly.

'Why?' he asked.

'You believe what you like, Richard,' she said.

He picked up the note. 'What am I supposed to believe?' he said.

Frankie looked up at him. 'Me,' she said.

7

Sylvia had rung David, just to make sure he was all right. She didn't know how she was going to tell him about this latest development. She was replacing the receiver as Richard came back in.

'Did you suspect?' he asked.

'Suspect what?' It wasn't merely to parry Richard's question.

'That Frankie was –' Richard looked embarrassed.

'Having an affair with Alan?' Sylvia finished for him. 'I don't really know,' she said. 'I find it difficult to accept.'

Richard sat down, and took out a cigar. 'Sylvia,' he said, 'I think you may have to accept it. I know how you must feel.'

'You don't know how I feel at all. Alan didn't have affairs, Richard. He was much too self-centred. He wanted to make a lot of money and become powerful, influential. Affairs are messy and dangerous, and someone else has the power. Alan would never put himself in that position.'

Richard looked distinctly uncomfortable. 'I think perhaps you're overestimating his will power,' he said.

But Sylvia shook her head. 'No,' she said. Poor Richard, wreathed in almost symbolic cigar smoke, had no chance whatever of penetrating the fog of Blake/O'Brien relationships. 'Frankie wouldn't do that,' she said. 'And – perhaps more to the point – Alan wouldn't have asked her to.'

When Richard still looked disbelieving, she tried to explain. 'I know what Frankie's like,' she said. 'She's a threat – don't misunderstand. I don't mean a conscious threat, but a threat all the same. She brings out the protective instinct in people. Not just in men – in women too. And that's when it gets dangerous, because how do you fight someone you're a little bit in love with yourself?' She smiled. 'You know what I mean. Everyone falls for her – everyone's looking out for Frankie.'

Richard nodded seriously. 'Mrs Milray,' he said thoughtfully. 'She told me to take care of her or else.'

'See what I mean?'

90

'Then why do you find it so difficult to believe?' he asked.

Sylvia thought for a moment. It wasn't difficult to believe. It was easy, it was so easy to believe.

'Perhaps I'm whistling in the dark,' she said.

The door opened and Frankie came in. 'I'm going now,' she said. 'You'll have to start your ulcers without me.'

Chapter Seven

1

The inquest had opened for identification and medical evidence to be heard. David had heard how his stepfather had been in generally good health and had been drinking on the evening of his death, which had occurred between the hours of nine and ten o'clock. He had fractured his skull and had died instantly. This was unusual, but not unheard of. Mr Blake had had a particularly thin skull and had struck his head on one of the stones as he fell. The fall itself would have been unlikely to have resulted in his death. There was a slight injury to his left cheekbone which had been caused by a blow which it was understood that Mr Blake had received during a violent altercation with his wife a little earlier in the evening.

David had heard his mother give evidence of identification, and in no time at all it was all over for a while as an adjournment was granted for further evidence to be produced.

Ashton the solicitor sat correctly in the armchair facing Sylvia, now that they had all come back from the Town Hall. He was dark and thin and was much more like David's idea of an undertaker than a solicitor. He had bundles of papers to which he referred now and again, which involved replacing his reading glasses, only to remove them again when he looked up at the assembly. The process was made the more complicated by his insistence on putting them away in their suede pouch each time.

Hascombe sat on the small sofa, a whisky on the coffee table which separated it from the large sofa on which Sylvia perched, as though it might burn her if she relaxed. She had had a dry sherry to keep him company, but she had left it untouched on the sideboard.

David sat by the glass and chrome chess table, turning the red queen over and over in his fingers, not really listening to Ashton, who seemed to be trying to say that the business was on the rocks in as many different ways as possible. He was asking for some papers.

'They'd be upstairs, I think,' Sylvia was saying.

'Perhaps you wouldn't mind if we took a look at them?' Ashton got to his feet and Sylvia reluctantly, cautiously, led the way to the study, throwing a glance over her shoulder at Hascombe, who nodded slightly.

David smiled shyly at Hascombe, who picked up his whisky and walked over to him.

'Do you play?' Hascombe asked, sitting opposite him and picking up one of the pieces. 'Beautiful set,' he said.

'No, sir. No-one does. Bl – my stepfather just bought it.'

'Whatever you do, please don't call me sir. It makes me feel like a schoolmaster.' He smiled.

'What should I call you?'

'Well, I thought you might call me Richard.'

David smiled politely, but he didn't think he could ever try that. He'd just have to call him nothing at all.

'Don't let Ashton get you down,' Hascombe said.

'But the business is in trouble?' David replaced the red queen. Was someone actually going to tell him something at last? All he knew was that Hascombe and Frankie had had some sort of bust-up, about which he could hardly feel sorry, and that there was something going on about the business.

'Yes, it's in trouble. But it might not be the end of the world. Your mother's decided to fight.' He sipped his whisky and soda.

He somehow managed to make it look like the most delicious whisky in the world. He made everything look intensely enjoyable, David thought. The whisky, the chessmen, his company, even.

'How much do you know about the business?' Hascombe asked.

'Not much. He didn't talk about it, and I didn't ask. I'm not really a businessman.'

'Do you want to know what we're doing?'

'Oh, of course,' David lied.

Hascombe took out a packet of cigars and held them up. 'Do you mind?' he asked.

'Not at all.'

He lit the cigar, and it looked like a most satisfying experience. At least this time David *knew* that it was one that he did not enjoy, however pleasant Hascombe made it look. As he spoke, David allowed his thoughts to wander to Frankie; he wondered what she was doing now.

2

Frankie was attempting some ineffectual tidying up, which she did by means of sweeping everything not immediately useful into any drawer or cupboard that had enough room to hold it. As she passed the cassette player, she pressed the Play button on the tape that was on, not knowing or caring what it was. It was satisfactorily raucous, and she turned up the volume in a gesture of defiance that immediately struck her as silly; she turned it back down to a more tolerable level. Her proper tape recorder was still at Richard's. She was glad; it symbolised the fact that the ties had not irretrievably been cut.

She began sorting out the newspapers that had accumulated on the answering machine. She opened last week's *Leader*, which lay, still folded as for pushing through a letter box, on the table. As she turned the pages, she saw Richard's face smiling urbanely and read the potted biography that some PR man had sent to the *Brampton Leader*.

... Mr Hascombe is a widower with one daughter, Amanda (25) who teaches in Hertfordshire ...

Frankie stuffed the paper into the plastic sack and consigned all the others to the same fate.

Leaving Blake's had seemed the only possible thing to do, but it was a frighteningly final step. She opened her bag and took out the note, shaking her head. She hadn't thought that even Alan could screw her life up from beyond the grave, but there it was. The note. It might have been carved in granite, so solidly did it stand between her and the life she had had just a week ago.

94

The knock at the door startled her; she put the note away and crossed the room, hoping that it wasn't Richard, who rang every day and left a message.

It wasn't Richard. Mrs Milray, looking cool and fresh despite the inordinate heat, stood on her doorstep.

'Oh, Christ,' was Frankie's greeting.

Mrs Milray smiled. 'You know, Frances, I'm always quite embarrassed by your effusive welcome.' She waited for Frankie to speak, but to no avail. 'May I come in?' she asked.

Frankie walked back into the room, leaving the door open.

Mrs Milray followed her in, closing the door.

3

David's attention was snapped back to Hascombe when he heard him talk of winding up the company.

'Are you going to?' he asked.

'I hope not.' The room was filling with cigar smoke and a sense of wellbeing. The smell reminded David of Christmas; spirits and cigars. It seemed wrong that outside the sun was beating down on the roses.

'Would you like another drink?' David asked, noticing that Hascombe's glass was empty.

'Thank you.'

David took the glass and went to the sideboard. He felt as though he ought to be asking questions, demanding some sort of proof of Hascombe's ability both to diagnose the problems and effect a cure. That there were problems he already knew from what Ashton had been saying. And that Hascombe could sort them out he knew because Hascombe said so.

Hascombe accepted his drink, and the shrewd grey eyes watched David for a moment.

'Is it all right?' David asked. 'Do you want more soda?'

'It's perfect,' he said, putting it down. 'David – you'll have gathered that your stepfather's death isn't as straightforward as it might be.'

David sat down. 'That's why the inquest was adjourned?' he asked.

95

'Yes. The police believe that he may have killed himself.'

'Killed *himself*?' The stress on the second word was accidental, instinctive; David hoped that Hascombe hadn't noticed. 'Why?'

'His life was in a bit of a mess,' Hascombe said. 'I've just told you about the firm – and you obviously know about his marital problems.'

David nodded. 'But even so,' he said.

'Yes,' Hascombe agreed. 'Even so.' He sipped his drink. 'But he left a note,' he said. 'To Frankie.'

David felt a little cold.

4

Mrs Milray had tendered her condolences, which had been accepted. Frankie had grudgingly offered her coffee and handed it to her.

'Thank you, dear,' she said. 'Now, as to why I've come. I understand you might be looking for a job?'

Frankie sat down. 'You're slipping,' she said. 'It's been almost a week.'

'Because I know of one,' Mrs Milray said, as though Frankie hadn't spoken. 'It's at the Centre – in the office. A little bit of everything – filing, typing, answering the phone – it doesn't pay all that well, but you do have an income of sorts from the houses, don't you?'

'Of sorts,' Frankie said. 'What Centre?'

'The Thompson Centre – the Trust set it up last year.'

Oh yes, thought Frankie. Mrs Milray's pet Trust. So she had got on the board at last.

'It mainly caters for unemployed people at the moment – it gives them a chance to do something more useful than stay at home and listen to pop music,' she said with a pointed glance at the speaker.

'Why don't you give the job to one of them?' Frankie asked.

'Because there isn't anyone suitable, dear. They're nearly all youngsters. There isn't anyone with your experience.'

96

Frankie smiled. 'And you think I'm suitable, do you? Do you want all these young persons exposed to me?'

'As long as you moderate your language, and don't seduce any of the instructors, I'm sure you'll get on famously,' said Mrs Milray. 'Are you interested?'

Frankie shrugged. She wasn't in the least interested, but it did have the edge on the dole queue as a way of passing the time. 'I'll go for the interview,' she said.

'No interview, Frances. The job's yours if you want it. Do you?'

'Why are you pulling strings to get me a job?' Frankie asked.

'Heaven knows, dear. You've always been entirely ungrateful.'

Frankie nodded. 'I do want it,' she said. 'And I'm not, you know.'

Mrs Milray was writing an address on a small pad. She tore out the sheet and handed it to Frankie. 'Not what, dear?' she asked.

'Not entirely ungrateful,' Frankie said.

5

Ashton and Sylvia came back, with Sylvia being too brittle and too bright, as she was when she was forced to speak. David handed her her sherry, in the hope it might relax her a little.

'I've found some more stuff,' his mother said, handing Hascombe a file of papers. 'In his desk drawer. I think that the top one's about that overdue order.'

Hascombe raised his eyebrows and opened the file. He took out the top sheet, laying it on the chess table, and frowned slightly as he read.

David could see the crossings-out, the margin notes, the arrows leading to scribbled afterthoughts and felt that it summed up his stepfather's character. Everything on the surface had to be neat and exact; it didn't matter what it looked like underneath. David could no more have produced a dog-eared piece of paper like that than he could have sprouted wings.

Hascombe began to smile, a reluctant, almost sad smile. He looked up. 'Frankie was right,' he said.

'About what?' Sylvia asked.

'That day we were all in the office – she said that I'd find a memo from Alan telling her what lies to tell about that order. Once you can make head or tail of it, that's what this is.'

Sylvia gave a short sigh. 'She knew Alan very well,' she said.

'Quite,' said Ashton, anxious to return to matters of more moment. 'Now, the immediate thing is to refute any suggestion of suicide at the inquest.'

'No,' Sylvia said quietly.

'But you do see, don't you, that there is the question of insurance?'

'The man from the insurance company said that he didn't foresee any difficulty,' Sylvia said.

'All the same,' Ashton pointed out. 'Mr Blake only took out the endowment mortgage ten months ago – and within a year of the policy being taken out, they would be within their rights to withhold payment.'

'But he said they wouldn't,' Sylvia said stubbornly.

'With respect, Mrs Blake,' Ashton said, 'it isn't up to him. He can only recommend. The company may not see it his way. If there is a suicide verdict, they could argue that he knew he wished to end his life when he took out the policy. I feel that you must try to get Miss O'Brien to say what the note means. Of course – she may confirm that it *is* a suicide note.'

Sylvia didn't speak or look at Ashton while he spoke, but David knew she was listening.

Hascombe spoke then, quietly. 'Sylvia,' he said. 'Are you saying you now believe that Alan did kill himself?'

'That's what it looks like,' she said quietly.

'You're agreeing with the police? About the meaning of the note?'

'I said that's what it looks like.'

6

'That's what it looks like,' Frankie said. 'But perhaps the inquest will prove that it wasn't.'

Mrs Milray finished her coffee. 'Perhaps,' she said. She looked across at Frankie. 'The rumour is –' she began.

'I know what the rumour is,' Frankie said.

'It's not true, is it?'

'No,' Frankie said miserably. 'Mrs Milray? Can I ask you a question?'

'Of course, dear.'

'You'll think it a bit strange,' she warned. 'I think you were the last person to leave Richard's barbecue?'

'Yes – I kept the poor man talking. And I think he really wanted to get away.'

Frankie smiled. 'Did a plane come over?' she asked. 'Flying very low?'

'Indeed one did!' Mrs Milray said crossly. 'It was quite iniquitous, over a built-up area. And not content with that, I was rudely awakened by another one that night. I rang the air base first thing next morning to complain, but all I got was a lot of soft soap about looking into it. They said there was only one plane – the second one was the first one coming back apparently. So I pointed out that in that event they would have no problem in having a word with the young man concerned.'

Only one plane. The final straw at which Frankie had been clutching had suddenly been ripped from her hand. How like Mrs Milray to answer a question that hadn't been asked. David's cartoon plane came into her mind, swooping over the little town, and there was no getting away from it.

Frankie decided on her course of action, and her shoulders drooped a little.

Mrs Milray stood up. 'Just go along on Monday,' she said. 'Tell them who you are and that I sent you.'

Frankie rose to show her out. 'Thank you,' she said.

'You're very welcome,' said Mrs Milray. She looked appraisingly at Frankie. 'It will get sorted out,' she said.

Frankie wasn't so sure. She gave a little shrug.

'In the meantime,' Mrs Milray said briskly, opening the door. 'There's an expression that seems to me to fit the occasion.' She turned back to face Frankie.

'Don't let the bastards grind you down,' she said, in her

99

expensively educated accent.

Frankie actually laughed.

7

'There is another explanation,' said Ashton. 'That the note was calling a halt to their relationship, let's say.'

David looked over at his mother, who frowned. 'Perhaps,' she said.

'The point is to prove that it needn't be a suicide note. If it isn't, then Miss O'Brien knows it and she has an obligation to say so.' Ashton started to put the papers into his brief case. 'And you have to try to prove it, Mrs Blake,' he said. 'Financially, you really have no choice. The insurance company are very far from making up their minds. They want to hear the evidence first. You do have your son's schooling to consider.'

Sylvia gave a long sigh. 'Do whatever you think is right,' she said.

The decision made, Ashton relaxed, and Hascombe gave a sympathetic, encouraging smile to Sylvia. She smiled back, grateful for the support, but she wasn't relaxing. She was as tense as a fighter coming out for the first round, David thought, and Frankie, of all people, was in the other corner.

Chapter Eight

1

Frankie rose early on the day that the inquest was to be resumed. She had seen every dawn since the night it all happened, but usually she just lay in bed, going over the details of the night, trying to find a different answer.

Today was the day, and she spent the pale early hours preparing for it. Outside the birds sang and called in the August sunshine, and the morning sounds began. The clink of milk being delivered and the whine of the milk-float in the empty morning street; next door's radio alarm, loudly playing music until he woke and turned it down; the car across the road that never started first time, but always spluttered into a semblance of life in the end. The steady build-up of traffic past her door, the morning paper, the mail.

The knock on the door was unexpected.

David stood on the step, his face determined and slightly flushed.

'Hello!' She stepped back. 'Are you sure it isn't bad luck to see the star witness on the morning of the inquest?'

David came in and stood uncertainly in the middle of the room. Frankie closed the door on the street-noises. 'Sit down,' she said. 'Would you like some coffee?'

'Yes please.'

Frankie went into the kitchen, where the best gadget she had ever bought was keeping the coffee hot. She poured two mugs and found some milk and sugar, which she put on a round tray that she wouldn't have known she possessed if anyone had asked her.

'Here we are,' she said, as the door swung to behind her.

'Don't do that' David said suddenly.

Frankie pushed the things on the coffee table over a bit, to

101

make room for the tray. 'Don't do what?' she asked.

'Sound all bright and breezy like that when you don't feel it. Mum's doing it.' he said.

'Sorry.' She knelt by the coffee table. 'One sugar, not much milk?'

'Yes, thanks.'

'How's your mother now?'

'Don't call her "your mother" as if you hardly knew her.'

'Is that why you've come? To tell me all the things I shouldn't do?' She handed him his coffee and sat back.

'Mum and Hascombe are at work. I wanted to talk to you.'

'Does she know you're here?'

'No.'

'I'm glad you came.'

David lifted large brown puppy eyes to hers. 'Are you going to work?' he asked.

'No. I've got the day off.'

'Do you like it? The new job?'

'Not much. It'll tide me over until I sort things out.'

'Will you – ?' He stared into his coffee. 'Will you be leaving Brampton?'

She couldn't see his face, just the shining brown hair, so like Sylvia's.

When she didn't answer straight away, he looked up. 'Will you?'

'I don't know, David. Things have just turned upside down. I might.'

The bleak look in his eyes upset her. 'It might not come to that,' she said. 'I just don't know.'

'Can I ask you something?'

'Sure.' Frankie drank some coffee.

'Something personal.'

'You can ask.'

'Is it true?' he asked at last. 'About you and him?'

Frankie sighed. 'No,' she said. 'No, it isn't true.'

A fascinating mixture of relief and disbelief crossed his features. 'Then why does everyone think that it is?' he asked.

'Who is everyone?' Frankie put down her mug.

'Mum and Hascombe. Even Mr Ashton.'

Her eyebrows rose. 'Have none of you anything better to do than discuss me?'

'I don't discuss you,' he muttered. 'Not really.'

'Anyway,' Frankie said. 'They're *not* everyone. Sylvia believes it, and they believe her.'

He pondered for a moment. 'But why?' he asked.

Frankie began to pick up the things that she had previously deposited on the floor. Pens, books, newspapers, a note pad. 'Alan wrote me a note,' she said, reluctantly. If she couldn't understand it, how could David? 'I don't know what it means, but they don't believe that.' She unloaded her collection on to the coffee table, knocking over David's empty mug, which he caught deftly.

'Well held!' she said, and the little incident had broken the inquisitorial atmosphere. David abandoned the conversation.

'Can I look for some books?' he asked, after a moment.

'Help yourself.'

'Thanks.' He walked over to the wall that Frankie had had shelved to accommodate all her books, but she still had overspill. He glanced through some of the ones piled up on the floor. 'How did you ever get that many books?' he asked.

'One good way is to borrow them and never give them back,' she said wickedly.

'Oh – sorry. I'll bring them back next time.'

He wandered along the shelves, his head on one side, while Frankie hunted through her cassettes and found the one she wanted, which was something of a stroke of luck. It was one of David's favourites, and she was rewarded with a smile. She sat on the floor again.

'David – how badly off is the firm? Do you know?'

David accepted the rapid change of subject without a blink. 'Pretty badly off,' he said. 'But Mr Hascombe might be able to sort something out, apparently.'

Frankie wondered. Would that have made Alan kill himself. The ignominy of failure? Would it have prompted that note?

David sat down with a small collection of books. 'That should keep me going,' he said.

'Shouldn't you be tearing round on a motorbike picking up girls?' Frankie asked.

'Probably,' he said.

'Have you got a girlfriend?'

He shrugged. 'No-one special.' He riffled through the top book. 'Will you wait for me?' he said with a laugh.

Frankie smiled. 'I might just do that,' she answered, standing up. 'More coffee?'

'Please.'

'I've a feeling you won't need me to wait,' she said from the kitchen, as she poured the coffee and laughed at the disbelieving noise from the living-room.

'I mean it,' she said, setting down the mugs. 'You're tall, dark and handsome, so you won't have too much trouble.' She sat cross-legged on the floor. 'And you're kind,' she said seriously. 'A lot of men aren't.'

'Like Blake, you mean.'

Frankie hadn't, particularly. 'He's an extreme example,' she said. 'There are more subtle ways of being unkind than using your fists.'

David's hand went to his eyes, too late to hide the tears that he swept away. 'I hated him,' he said with a simplicity that brooked no argument.

But Frankie had no desire to argue. 'Well,' she said quietly. 'It's over.'

They finished their coffee in silence, and David took the mugs into the kitchen. Frankie tried some more unsuccessful tidying up.

'I've washed the dishes,' he said, when he emerged.

'Oh – thank you. You didn't have to.'

He looked round the room. 'Someone had to,' he said.

'Cheeky!'

'Swear to God it isn't true,' he said suddenly.

Frankie shook her head. 'I don't believe in God,' she said. 'I've told you it isn't. That's the best you're going to get.'

'I saw him,' he said.

Frankie stared at him. 'What?'

'Blake.' He sat down on the sofa, his eyes fixed firmly on the

104

floor. 'Leaving here,' he said.

Frankie mentally heaved a sigh of relief. 'What about it?' she asked. 'He was always here. He got me that answering machine and then only used it to say he was on his way over.'

'It was when I went back to school,' he said. 'After half-term.'

'Sorry, David. You'll have to give me more clues.'

David muttered something that she couldn't catch and she bent her head down. 'What did you say?'

'I said the coach leaves Brampton at half past seven in the morning,' he repeated, dragging his eyes from the floor to look at her. 'He'd had a fight with Mum and hadn't come home, and I saw him leaving here.'

Frankie stepped back and regarded him. She could obey her instincts and tell him that what went on in her house was her business and that she had had more than enough of defending herself against sudden, unprovoked attacks on her integrity. Or she could tell him what he wanted to know.

'You probably did,' she said. 'And he slept where you're sitting.'

David dropped his gaze. 'Are you angry?' he asked.

'Yes,' she said. 'But, if you must know, I came home and found him sleeping off *my* booze. So I told Sylvia where he was and threw a blanket on him.' She tapped his shoulder. 'All right?' she asked.

'Sorry,' he said. 'I'd better go.'

'I think you should.'

He opened the door and turned back. 'I couldn't *help* wondering,' he said. 'I'm sorry.'

'Forget it,' Frankie said.

He smiled, and left.

2

The police had said that their enquiries had revealed that the deceased had been under considerable financial strain and had had a violent argument with his wife earlier in the evening. His car was found, unlocked, on the old quarry road. The keys were in the ignition and a note had been found, addressed to 'Frankie', whom they now knew to be Frances O'Brien, a friend and colleague. Nothing else was found in the car.

Richard was in the restaurant of the Bull, trying to persuade Sylvia to eat something. The worst, after all, was over. They had done their best. Sylvia looked at him when he said that as though he had just kicked her puppy. But her part was over, he argued, ordering for her.

She had given her evidence, looking, as the paper would almost certainly say, pale and composed. The coroner had spoken gently to her for a moment or two, to try to put her at ease, but with little apparent success.

No, her husband had never spoken about suicide, either personally or generally.

No, he had not been at home that afternoon. He had left the house at about 2.30 p.m. He had not said where he was going. No, this was not unusual. He often left without saying exactly where he was going. He had gone into his office, they now knew.

Miss O'Brien was a close family friend and had been her husband's assistant. She had now left the firm.

Yes, her husband had become violent during a row while they were attending a party at a friend's house.

No, it had never happened before.

Yes, he was obviously under a strain, but she did not believe that he would kill himself.

No, she did not think that the note was a suicide note.

Richard ordered for David too, who had said nothing whatever since they had left the Town Hall.

The verdict would be suicide. Frankie still said that she didn't know what the note meant, but she didn't deny any suggestion of suicide.

3

Mark was hungry; Joyce seemed to regard this as the height of insensitivity, but nevertheless accompanied him to the café across from the Town Hall. She stopped as they got to the door.

'It's Frankie,' she said. 'She's there.'

'Perhaps we should go somewhere else,' Mark said.

'No! She'll think we're trying to avoid her,' Joyce said. 'She could do with some moral support.'

'Of course she won't think we're avoiding her,' Mark said. 'And she knows she's got moral support. I'm sure she'd rather be alone.'

Joyce shook her head. 'You mean you don't want to talk to her in case she gets upset,' she said.

It was true, of course. Mark had been dragooned into going to the inquest at all. He really didn't need to watch Sylvia and Frankie to know what they were going through. He had listened to the contents of the much talked about note without a flicker of interest showing on his face, but he had found the whole thing unbelievable. Alan, the archetypal cold fish, and Frankie, with her white-hot emotions, seemed inconceivable. But they said that opposites attract, and he and Joyce weren't soul-mates, come to that.

They went in and he was relieved to see Frankie leave money on the table to pay for her half-eaten hamburger. She left by the other door, pretending she hadn't seen them.

'I told you she wouldn't want company,' he said, after the waitress took his order.

'Poor Frankie,' Joyce said.

Mark didn't really want to think about it. But the note nagged at him. It didn't make any sense.

Oh well, he thought, as he unwrapped his knife and fork from the paper napkin, maybe it made sense to Frankie.

'Doesn't any of this affect you at all?' Joyce asked.

He speared a chip. 'No point,' he said.

But he felt for Frankie, who had looked so young and defenceless as she had given her evidence.

Yes, Frankie had said, *the note had read like a suicide note.*

No, she did not understand the reference to starting all over again, unless he meant the business.

No, she did not know what he meant by 'running out' on her.

Yes, she understood the importance of these proceedings.

No, she did not understand the note.

Yes, he obviously thought she knew what he meant, but she did not.

Yes, she had said that it read like a suicide note. That was not her first thought upon reading it, but it did read like one. She had wondered if it was because the business was in financial difficulties.

She didn't know why he would write it to her, except that they worked together.

No, she was a friend of the family, not especially of Mr Blake's.

Yes, she understood that it was the purpose of the inquest to arrive at the truth.

No, it was not possible that Mr Blake was merely ending their relationship when he wrote the note. They had not had the sort of relationship that could be ended in this fashion.

Yes, she was maintaining that she did not understand the note, but that it read like a suicide note and that it could have been about the business.

Yes, it read as though Mr Blake had taken his own life.

Frankie had looked only at the coroner and Sylvia's counsel as she had given her answers. Poor little Frankie, battling both of them. Pale, thin and unhappy, but hanging in there. And Mark had been affected by it all. But there was no point in shouting it from the rooftops. It couldn't help.

All that they could do now was go back to hear the coroner's summing up and the verdict.

4

The verdict was suicide. It didn't matter much to Frankie, who sat motionless while everyone shuffled out of the stuffy room. Whichever way it had gone, she would still have been the villain of the piece. She rose and walked along the corridor out into the late afternoon sunshine. But there was no time to breathe a sigh of relief that it was over, because there was no chance of its being over.

David was waiting for her. 'Why?' he asked. 'Why didn't you just tell me the truth?'

Frankie was tired. Too tired to argue any more.

'You know that it wasn't a suicide note,' he said. 'You *know* that, and you let them believe it was. Mum will lose everything.'

Sylvia came up behind him and Frankie saw the look on her

face, a look she knew well.

'Oh, Frankie,' she said in the same tone she had used when Frankie, at seventeen, had thought she was pregnant. A despairing tone. 'What have you done?'

'Nothing,' she said helplessly. 'Nothing. I've done nothing.' But Sylvia and David had walked away, and she realised that she had spoken the words to herself.

She had never felt so alone, so defeated. There were no new words to protest her innocence, only the same inadequate ones. You couldn't keep saying them for ever, if no-one would listen. She felt suddenly, desperately weary.

5

Despite himself, David kept sneaking looks at Frankie during the service. He knew Frankie's feelings about funeral services – she had only come to prove some sort of a point. She was on her own, standing a little way away from the Rainfords.

She looked too pale, and too thin, and as though she hadn't been sleeping properly. David tried hard to think that it served her right, but he couldn't. His mother stood beside him, tight-lipped and trembling slightly. Why did the two people he cared most about in the world have to suffer because of someone like Blake?

Despite everything, he still found it hard to believe. Frankie couldn't have done a thing like that. He tried to imagine it, until he was assailed by the notion that there was something definitely wicked about doing that in what was, after all, a church. Even if it was only the one at the crematorium. He felt his face grow hot and hoped that no-one had noticed.

But the thought wouldn't go away entirely. She was Frankie. She wasn't like anyone else. At sixteen, the purity of David's childhood feelings was being eroded by adolescent desire, and the hurt was immeasurably worse. He was realistic enough to know that there would be men in her life, but not Blake. Never Blake. Hascombe was bad enough – but *Blake*. He looked at her again, when he was supposed to be praying for his stepfather's soul, to try to make himself believe it. The mint-green eyes caught his, and he looked away quickly.

He didn't really believe that he could ever have Frankie for himself, but there had always been the dream, the ghost of a chance. There were girls his own age, girls he saw from time to time, but they didn't measure up. One of them had satisfied his curiosity, but she hadn't satisfied him; Frankie had remained the ideal, the ultimate goal.

Outside, in the cloud-filtered sunshine, people stood in murmuring groups while his mother spoke to the vicar.

As the soft, fine rain began to fall, Frankie walked away, and he wanted with all his being to go after her; instead, he walked to the waiting car.

The cars picked up a little speed once they left the town, David was thankful to discover, as they set off for home. By the time they reached the Caswells, the shower had eased off and watery sunshine glinted off the rain on the leaves outside. David escaped from the drawing-room, where everyone was talking about anything but what had happened.

Out in the garden, he breathed in the fresh air and walked along the curving crazy-paving to the rose garden, surrounded by the precarious dry-stone wall that he constantly had to rebuild owing to his lack of expertise. His mother kept threatening to have it removed, but he enjoyed building it, and would have been very disappointed if it hadn't always fallen down again. He found himself appraising the latest breach, working out what size and shape of stones he wanted, until he realised guiltily that he was cheerfully contemplating fetching stones from the quarry. It was difficult to remember to mourn Blake, even on the day of his funeral. The rain-heightened scent of the roses lifted him a little; his feet squelched on the grass paths as he walked round, trying to remember their names, until the sun had dried the bench, and he could sit down. He had never felt so confused in his life.

He had always been so sure of Frankie. If you asked her a question, she answered it without preamble and without the fuss and the hedging that other people used to disguise the truth. He had believed her and she had been lying. That morning was cocooned in his memory, like a living, breathing photograph.

How she had looked, how she had sounded, how she had smelt. But the afternoon was there as well, the afternoon of the very same day, when everything had shattered. And Blake must have sat in her untidy room too. She must have made him coffee and said nice things to him. She must have played the music *he* liked, and let him – he screwed up his eyes to shut the images out, but he couldn't.

There was a noise as someone came into his sanctuary.

'They've gone,' Hascombe was saying. 'And I'm on my way, too. Your mother asked me to tell you.'

'Thank you,' he said.

'You feel as if you've just been to Frankie's funeral, don't you?' Hascombe asked with devastating accuracy. 'Well you haven't. She's a survivor, David. Remember that.'

6

Frankie had gone back to work after the funeral, but the afternoon hadn't seemed real. She had worked on automatic pilot until the clock said she could go home.

She hadn't trusted herself to drive and had left the car at home. Now, she could barely trust herself to walk. One foot in front of the other. Once she was home, it would be all right. People walked past her quickly, people whose heads didn't hurt. People who could cross the road, running through the Friday night traffic. People who could look both ways. She could only look straight ahead and take one step at a time.

But one step at a time works, in the end. She was there, stepping through the front door of the untidy, neglected house that had become a cool oasis in a hostile desert. The venetian blinds shaded the room, and she liked the semi-darkness, hiding her from the rest of the world, from all those people.

But even as she shut the door, she realised that one of them was in there with her.

Chapter Nine

1

She could just make out a figure, rising from the sofa at the back of the room. She supposed she ought to be alarmed, but she was too exhausted. She was aware of the pain behind her eyes and acute tiredness. Nothing more. 'If you're a burglar,' she said, 'please don't take the coffee-maker.'

Richard came into the slatted half-light.

'Oh Christ, no.' Frankie had nothing left. No more words. She let her bag drop on to the chair.

'You don't look well,' Richard said.

Frankie sat down and removed her bag from where it dug into the small of her back. 'Go away,' she said, leaning her head against her hand, trying to rub away the pain.

'I can't let you carry on like this,' he said.

It hurt to speak. 'You don't *let* me do anything,' she said. She longed for a cup of coffee. 'Go away. Go and look after Sylvia.' She was speaking between the regular beats of pain.

'Well, it might not be much in the way of conversation,' Richard said, 'But it's better than that recorded message. Why didn't you answer my calls?' Without waiting for a reply, he walked briskly towards the kitchen. 'I've made coffee,' he said.

Frankie could have forgiven him then and there. He came out with a mug of steaming, strong, life-saving liquid.

'Hot,' he said, as if she were a toddler.

Frankie blew the steam. 'Why are you here?' she asked.

'God knows.'

'Do you still want to hit me?' Her head throbbed and she spoke with difficulty. She drank some coffee and looked across at Richard, who had sat down again.

'I think that's probably a chronic condition,' he said. 'But it's

112

not why I'm here.'

'Then what do you want?' Every word resounded in her head.

'I think you should come back with me,' he said. 'Now that it's all over.'

'All over?' Frankie got to her feet, but the action made her dizzy and she stumbled. Richard was at her side, steadying her. Her head had acquired a separate, pulsating identity as she straightened up.

'You've lost weight,' he said. 'You didn't have enough to start with. Take something for your headache and come back with me.'

It was a headache. Oh yes, of course, that's what it was. It wasn't a part of her, something she had been born with and had to live with. It was a headache. It would go away again.

'It's not over,' she said. 'Someone knows what that note means. Someone wanted it to look like suicide.'

Richard let her go. 'Is that what you think?' he asked.

Frankie wasn't aware of thinking anything. She was existing, reacting. Her head hurt much too much to think.

'What?' she said.

'Do you think someone *killed* him?'

'Yes,' she said, vaguely surprised at the question. It had never occurred to her that anyone thought otherwise.

'Did you say that to the police?'

'No.' Frankie felt suddenly weak. It was almost possible to regard the pain as someone else's, as though she could step away from it, forget about it, float away from it. Just float away from it.

'Are you all right?'

Richard's voice sounded as though he were speaking from the bottom of a well. She was back in the armchair, raising her head from between her knees.

'How do you feel now?' he asked.

She could feel beads of perspiration on her forehead and upper lip. She felt cold. She felt a little sick.

'Fine,' she said.

2

David lay on his bed, trying to work people out. Frankie – nice, straightforward Frankie, had lied to him. His mother, who should be angry, seemed to understand, even to sympathise with her. More than that; she was worried about her, worried *for* her, though David had no idea why. Hascombe apparently thought everything could be sorted out, but that was his attitude to everything. So far nothing much seemed to be getting sorted out.

There was a knock on the door. He sat up on the bed. 'Come in,' he said.

His mother opened the door. 'Are you all right?' she asked.

'Of course,' he said.

'Did the funeral upset you?' She came into the room.

'No,' he said.

'You're not worrying about me, are you?' she said, sitting beside him. 'Because you mustn't.'

He didn't answer.

'It's just a house. We'll sell it – it's too big for us anyway. I don't think we'll lose money. A smaller house will have fewer outgoings. And the company could get back on its feet.' She smiled. 'I think social security's a little way off. Besides, I think we'll get the insurance, whatever Ashton says.'

None of this had done more than cross his mind, and David realised guiltily that he had been being selfish.

'Is it school? We'll be able to keep you there even if we don't get the insurance. I've had an offer of a loan.'

'No,' he said. 'It's not school.' He looked up at his mother, at her concerned, tired face. 'How could Frankie do that?'

His mother put her arm round his shoulders. He wished he didn't find it so comforting. He wasn't a child.

'It happens,' she said.

'But Frankie!'

His mother's arm tightened on his shoulders.

'She's no different from everyone else,' she said.

'She was,' he said.

114

'No. You believed she was, that's all. If you put people on pedestals, they'll always disappoint you.'

'It's all her fault.'

'No, it's not.' She hugged him. 'I was shocked too,' she said. 'I couldn't believe it either. But perhaps it was inevitable, in a way. Frankie's no saint, you know, David. And she needs drama.' She was speaking almost to herself. 'Alan and I weren't exactly a conventional married couple. She was there every day, working with him. Perhaps understanding him better than I did. I can imagine the circumstances appealing to Frankie's sense of theatre.'

David was shocked. 'She shouldn't have let it happen!'

'Probably not. But she needs an older man, and Alan was there. And other people have to take some of the blame. I have to. Alan has to.'

'Why are you taking her side?'

She smiled a little sadly. 'I'm not. But everyone's hurt everyone else. I wish you hadn't got caught in the crossfire.'

David shook his head. 'But she let everyone believe it was suicide!' He tried to understand, but no-one seemed to stay in the same place for long. 'And she lied to me. She lied to everyone. She's like a different person,' he said, 'ever since it happened. Why was she like that with the police?'

Sylvia sighed. 'Let me tell you something about Frankie,' she said.

3

Frankie had eaten, albeit only cornflakes, and those with marked reluctance. The colour was at last returning to her cheeks and the freckles fading. Richard watched her as she took the last mouthful, like a fond father encouraging baby to eat.

It seemed reasonable to ask again. He didn't imagine that it was the actual question which had made her faint.

'Why didn't you tell the police?'

She shrugged. 'Tell them what?' she asked. 'That I have a feeling in my bones that Alan was killed?' She poured the inevitable coffee.

'That won't help you relax,' he said.

'I don't *want* to relax.' She pushed a mug towards him. 'And anyway, I don't know who killed him.'

Richard smiled. 'I don't think they would expect the full Sherlock Holmes,' he said.

Frankie's level gaze met his. 'That's not what I mean,' she said. 'All I really know is that *that* – 'she picked up the dog-eared note. ' – isn't a suicide note. For one thing, Alan wouldn't kill himself and, if he did, he wouldn't write to me about it. But –' she talked down the protest that had risen to his lips. 'But, he *might*. But if he did, he'd write something that I could understand. And he didn't. He wrote a note full of crocodile tears about something I know nothing about.'

'But how? You're not saying he didn't write it?'

'I'm sure he wrote it. And he wrote it to me. But it ought to make sense, and it doesn't.'

'He was drunk.'

'Not that drunk.'

'No,' Hascombe agreed.

'And someone has used it. To make it look like suicide. Don't you see? That has to be someone I know.'

Hascombe's eyebrows rose. 'Who?'

'If I knew that, we wouldn't be in this mess,' she said. 'Anyone. We all turned up at the scene of the crime, like a detective story. But it was like starting at the wrong end. All the suspects were gathered together before we knew anyone was dead.' She massaged her forehead. 'And we forgot to bring the butler, and that's the problem, isn't it? Because it must have been one of us.'

A shiver went down his back, as he looked at the note, spread out on the table. Written on cheap, lined paper, with a corner missing, it looked ordinary, innocuous. It didn't look as though it could disrupt lives.

He frowned a little. 'Is that the original note?' he asked.

'Yes,' said Frankie. 'They gave it to me once the inquest was over. Why?'

'Oh – nothing. I just wondered.'

For a moment, he had felt as though he'd seen it before. Not at the inquest, where he wouldn't have known if they had been passing round a shopping list, but like it was now, lying on the table. But he couldn't have, he told himself, and put it down to a moment's déjà-vu.

4

David wouldn't look at her; Sylvia wasn't sure if she should have told him at all.

'I don't remember any of that going on,' David said. He stared at his feet.

'You were only five,' Sylvia said. She smiled. 'I remember you asking me if Frankie had been naughty.'

'She had,' he said primly.

Yes, thought Sylvia. She had. She remembered the terrible evening that she had spent with Frankie when her father died, and the aching sense of responsibility that she had felt then came back. She had been too involved with a sick man and a small boy to notice that Frankie needed her too. She had blamed herself for what had happened then. So how could she blame Frankie for what was happening now?

'Don't you hate her?' he asked. 'For doing this?'

'No. I'm just a little frightened for her. She lives on the very edge, all the time. She feels things too violently.'

'But why aren't you angry?' he asked.

Sylvia looked at him, her head slightly to one side as though she were appraising a painting.

'We have two different points of view,' she said. 'I don't really care if Frankie stole Alan.' She patted him. 'But you're angry because Alan stole Frankie.'

She rose as she heard a call from downstairs. 'Mrs Mac's leaving,' she said. 'I have to pay her.' She stopped at the door. 'Are you coming down?'

'Not yet,' he said.

Mrs Mac was putting her coat on. 'That's it, Mrs Blake,' she said. 'I'll see you on Monday.'

'Thank you.' Sylvia handed over Mrs MacKenzie's wages and

wondered if she could still afford to do so.

She began devising the meal that was to tempt David down from his bedroom.

She had never known Frankie really to lie before, but she was so single-minded, so determined, that she could imagine that she would stick to a lie to the bitter end once she'd told one. She had decided that she wasn't going to say what the note meant, and that was that.

Sylvia produced tempting dishes with the exaggerated care of acquired rather than natural skill, giving herself over to rescuing her son from his first major disillusionment. Food could usually be relied upon to help.

5

David was sketching, headphones clamped to his ears, making drawing after drawing and scoring through them almost as soon as he'd finished. He turned the music up, so that it pounded in his ears, but it didn't stop him thinking.

And if there was a tiny doubt creeping into his mind that his image of Frankie might have been a trifle idealised, he sent it packing. With every stroke of his pencil, through every drawing, he sent it packing.

The last few weeks had turned everything on its head. Was Frankie really a cheat and a liar? Was she really afraid to admit what she'd done? No. Because whatever else she may be, Frankie wasn't a coward. She had stood her ground at the inquest, answering question after question, and breaking his heart, because she was taking them all on and she was losing and still she didn't give an inch.

His mind went again to the painting, the painting that still wasn't finished, because it needed Frankie. The sole survivor. Hascombe was right. Frankie was a survivor.

6

Frankie's head had settled down to a dull ache as she relaxed in the comfort of Richard's car, on her way back to Long Caswell. It was cooler now that Friday night clouds were ringing the sky, heralding another wet weekend, and her eyelids began to droop as she enjoyed the sensation of the breeze on her face.

Through half-opened eyes, she could see the horizon, hazy with smoke from burning stubble, and in the distance a sloping field striped with fire. As the lines of flame advanced in diagonal formation across the ground, she could smell the smoke and feel the heat from the crackling, snapping fires.

The controlled, contained destruction touched something within her, but the moment fled before it could be recognised. She blamed the smoke for the tear in her eye and wound up the window.

The car slowed down as they caught up with a tractor trailing a lethal farm implement. 'I think you should talk to Sylvia,' Richard said.

'Do you?' Frankie watched as the tractor turned shakily off the road up a farm track. 'I think she thinks –' she shook her head. 'Never mind. Thinking isn't good enough. You have to *know*.'

Richard picked up speed. 'You have more than just a feeling in your bones,' he said. 'Haven't you?'

'Yes.'

'Tell me.'

She closed her eyes again. 'No,' she said. 'I'm not saying anything until I know.'

There was silence, but she didn't open her eyes to look at him. If she did, she would have to guess at what was going on in his mind.

He cleared his throat. A little nervously? She put the thought out of her mind and kept her eyes closed to avoid the temptation to observe Richard's reactions. She would have to soon enough, if she took the course she was plotting. But it didn't have to start yet.

'Do you mean that someone told a lie?' he asked.

She opened her eyes to see him glance quickly at her. 'Why are you smiling?' he asked.

Frankie didn't really know. She could barely remember the last time she had smiled, and there was nothing whatever to smile about.

'Everyone told lies,' she said. 'The odd thing is that someone told the truth.'

Chapter Ten

1

It was raining hard when Frankie's eyes opened.

She had been marking time for weeks, looking forward to the moment when everything would be behind her and the cold dread would be gone. But it hadn't gone at all, and she came to reluctant consciousness, listening to the rain falling fast and hard past the open window. Perhaps she could have accepted that it was all over, as it ought to have been, had she not hardened into words her certainty that Alan had been killed. But she had, and there was no way back from there.

From downstairs, the soft chimes of the sitting-room clock began. Eight, nine, ten, eleven. She sat up, disoriented. It couldn't be eleven. It was daylight and it had been dusk when she had fallen into bed, too tired, too angry, too frustrated to think straight any more. She couldn't remember waiting for sleep; she couldn't remember dreaming. But it *was* daylight, and it was eleven o'clock. It had to be the next day, and she felt cheated of the time she'd lost, of which she knew nothing. She began to gather about her the things she did know, but there was, she realised, little comfort to be had there.

She was in Richard's bed, but nothing had been resolved. She had agreed to come back with him only because she had had no strength left to argue. During the evening she had become acutely aware that amnesty was being given to her, and the indignation which had begun to smoulder on the road back to the Caswells had been given sudden and harsh expression, culminating in an inelegantly succinct demand to be left alone. It had had the desired effect; Richard had left, she had gone to bed and the world had got itself through the night and most of the morning with no help from her.

She had violated a ceasefire to which she had never agreed and she wondered, just a little bitterly, if she was being forgiven for that, too.

2

Richard smiled his thanks to Mrs Rogers, who had arrived in his study with morning coffee before the eleventh chime had faded.

'Should I take one up to Miss O'Brien?' she asked.

'If you like,' Richard said, regretting his obvious childish sulkiness even as he spoke the words. 'Yes, do, please. She takes it black, without sugar.' Mrs Rogers turned to go. 'In a mug,' he said as an afterthought. 'She drinks it by the gallon.'

Mrs Rogers nodded and left.

Richard pushed away the columns of figures that were beginning to dance on the page and rubbed his eyes. He had not slept well.

He had gone to see Sylvia last night, when Frankie had made it so abundantly clear that his company was not to her taste. And he had come back at midnight, not knowing whether she would still be there or not. She hadn't stirred when he had joined her and when he had been wakened by the thunderstorm that tore the night apart, she had carried on sleeping without so much as a flicker of her eyelashes.

The thunder had continued to roll around the sky after its first ferocity had died down and every rumble, every blink of lightning, had roused him from what he chose to regard as sleep. But not Frankie, who might have been dead, were it not for her regular breathing. If he could have hated her, it would have been then.

He had looked in during the morning, but she had still been sleeping her dead, exhausted sleep, and he had wondered, for a moment, if she were ill. But her forehead was cool, despite the dark strands of hair clinging to it. The rain had done nothing to cool the heavy atmosphere; he had pushed up the window to admit more of what passed for air and for the first time her eyelids had opened slightly to reveal delicate sightless green and closed again immediately.

He sighed and drank his rapidly cooling coffee, returning once more to his figures when he heard the faint knock that preceded her half entrance. She stood in the doorway, her hand on the knob, dark circles under her too-bright eyes. The long, unbroken sleep which might have restored her seemed only to have made her more brittle.

'You're going to listen to me,' she said, and her voice shook. Her hand gripped the door-knob like a life line.

'Am I?' He put down his pen and leant back in the chair. 'In that case, I hope you can rise to less basic language than you were using yesterday.'

She abandoned the door and walked into the room. 'If it takes basic language to make you understand, then that's what I'll use,' she said.

Richard pushed back his chair, walking round his desk to close the door. He didn't know what he had expected. Possibly contrition, but that had just been a vague fantasy. Possibly sheepish acceptance that her outburst had been uncalled for, but that had obviously been wishful thinking. What he hadn't expected was the same, unabated, quivering anger that he had left last night.

She was holding the back of a chair with white-knuckled intensity, waiting for him to get back into her line of vision. When he did so, her eyes burned at him.

'Well?' he said. 'What have I to listen to?'

'I won't be forgiven for something that I did not do,' she said. The last three words were spaced out with pauses. 'Do you understand?'

'Yes,' he said. 'No need to resort to Anglo-Saxon thus far.' He was sparring with her, his pomposity making her angrier than ever. And he was glad, because her crude dismissal of him had shocked him, and it still stung.

He waved a hand at the chair she was clutching. 'Why don't you sit down?' he asked, seating himself behind his desk again, where he felt safer and more at home.

She shook her head and waited until he had lit his cigar before she spoke again.

'Sylvia –' she began, and faltered. She took a deep breath. 'Sylvia means more to me than anyone else I know. She's done more *for* me than anyone else I know. I owe her a great deal, and I did not repay her by going to bed with her husband.' She looked at him unblinkingly through the smoke that drifted round her. 'Is that clear? Because if it isn't, there is absolutely no point in my staying here.'

It was clear. And obviously the truth. He nodded. 'Sit down,' he said, his tone as conciliatory as he could make it, given that he was still angry. 'Please.'

She released the back of the chair and relaxed visibly. 'Thank you,' she said, sitting down.

'But isn't it more important to make Sylvia understand?' he asked.

She shook her head.

Richard drew on his cigar. Between them, Sylvia and Frankie had utterly confused him. 'Why not?' he ventured.

'Because she doesn't think I did,' she said. She leant forward, her hands on the desk. 'She knows me – and she knew Alan – too well. So,' she said, 'just for the record – Alan never once even made a pass at me nor, as far as I'm aware, at anyone else.'

He reached across the desk to touch her hand, but she took it away.

'Before that note ever made an appearance,' she said, 'you asked me if there was anything between me and Alan. Why?'

Richard gave himself time to think, for how could he set the fire-breathing Frankie on poor young David, whose naked adoration of her had caused him to make an unguarded aside which no-one was really meant to hear?

'Just something I overheard,' he answered truthfully. 'I must have misconstrued it,' he added with less truth.

But she remained expectantly leaning forward.

He crushed out the cigar. 'It's the truth,' he said.

But it was all or nothing with Frankie, and she remained unmoved.

'All right, I didn't misconstrue it,' he admitted. 'But the speaker was obviously mistaken. It wasn't said maliciously, and I'm not going to tell you who it was. I really don't want you to go kicking anyone's teeth down their throat today.'

She sat back, regarding him cautiously, like a cat.

'What difference does it make who said it?' he asked, unnerved by her silence.

She didn't seem to be going to answer. Richard picked up his pen and resumed his contemplation of the more exact science of Blake's accounts. After a few moments, he looked up to find Frankie still apparently watching him, but her mind far away.

'The property side isn't at all bad,' he remarked conversationally. 'Of course, he had too many plates spinning at once – he should have made up his mind whether he was in property or electronics.'

Frankie looked at him vaguely. 'He liked to have his finger in a lot of pies,' she said.

'He knew what he was doing in Westbridge,' Richard said, keeping the conversation going now that she had actually spoken. 'He was in the right place at the right time once or twice. Unless it was just luck.'

Frankie shrugged. 'He probably had a councillor in his pocket,' she said uncharitably.

Richard smiled. 'Perhaps.'

Frankie stood up. 'Are you really not going to tell me who said whatever it was that you overheard?'

'Really,' Richard said. 'And I don't see why it should be important to you.'

'Don't you?' Frankie asked. 'Someone wanted Alan's death to look like suicide,' she said. 'So they planted that note. But they wanted *me* to believe it, didn't they? They didn't want me making waves. And if they thought I'd believe it, then they presumably thought that Alan and I were having an affair. That's why it's important,' she said. 'Because Alan Blake's dead, and everyone thinks I drove him to it.'

'I don't,' he reminded her. 'Not any more.'

'No,' she said. 'You don't. Mark does, and Joyce. David does – and perhaps Sylvia thinks something even worse than that. Mrs Rogers does. Mrs Milray does.' She paused. 'Sergeant Dempster.'

Richard frowned, his grey eyes perplexed. 'But you –' he stopped. 'At the inquest,' he said. 'Why did you say you thought

125

it was a suicide note?'

'Because,' she said, looking past him, out of the window, 'I thought I knew who had done it. I don't know now. I'm not sure any more.' She looked back at him. 'But I'm going to find out,' she said.

Richard sighed. 'It was just an accident, Frankie,' he said. 'Forget it, for God's sake.'

'I can't forget it,' she said. 'I'm going to find out what really happened.'

Richard's heart sank as he realised the futility of trying to stop her. But he *did* have to try. 'That's the police's job,' he said. 'Not yours.'

'No. *I'm* the one he wrote that letter to – not the police. It must mean something and someone *knows* what it means. Someone did this to me, and I'm going to find out who.' She looked at him defiantly. 'Why shouldn't I?'

'Because,' he said slowly, 'if you are right, then it could be dangerous. Don't you see? You've just said that everyone thinks Alan killed himself. But if you're right, then someone knows perfectly well that he didn't. And you can't be sure who to trust.'

He had expected scorn. He had expected her to ridicule the notion, to laugh. Instead, she looked steadily at him, her face serious.

'I know,' she said.

Again, the shiver of apprehension went down his back.

'But I'm going to find out,' she said again, with a dreadful finality. She stood up and left the room.

Richard stayed looking at the closed door for some moments after she had gone.

It would be so easy to rouse Frankie's passions, to make her run blindly into danger, and over the edge. So easy.

3

Joyce looked anxiously at the clock, then tried to look as though she hadn't, when she realised that Mark had seen her.

'It's all right,' he said. 'I won't slope off when your back's

126

turned.' It was said without rancour.

'I'm sorry.' Joyce dried the last plate and lifted the dish-drainer to wipe the work-top. She too was making a conscious effort; her hand automatically reached out for the squeegee to give the floor a going-over and she arrested it. She left the kitchen before she thought of anything else. Mark had left a newspaper on the dining table, she noticed, and a tea cup on the storage radiator, but she sat down resolutely on the sofa.

'I met your friend Mrs Milray this morning,' she said.

'She's not my friend,' Mark complained mildly.

'Well, she knows you and you know her,' Joyce said.

'That makes her an acquaintance.'

'Right. I met your acquaintance Mrs Milray this morning,' she said. 'She says that Richard's sorting out Alan's personal business for Sylvia.'

Mark nodded. 'I thought he might,' he said. 'He seems to be getting his feet under the table there.'

'That's not what's bothering me,' Joyce said.

'I know. But you don't have to worry. Honestly.' He smiled. 'I've told you,' he said. 'Worrying takes all the fun out of not being dead yet.'

Joyce pulled a face. 'Anyway, you're wrong about Richard and Sylvia,' she said. 'Mrs Milray says that Frankie's back with Richard. She stayed there last night.'

Mark grinned. 'Has that woman got radar?'

'I don't think she needs it,' Joyce said. 'She'd have been an asset to the Gestapo. Mrs Rogers had just left the shop, so I suppose she gave more than her name, rank and number.' Her face sobered. 'Do you think it's true about Frankie and Alan?' she asked.

The lazy grin appeared again on Mark's face. 'The question is,' he said, 'does Mrs Milray?'

'Seriously, though,' she said. 'Do you?'

'I am being serious. She seems to be a very reliable source.' He stood up. 'I'm for a beer. Do you want one?'

Joyce shook her head.

'That note doesn't leave much room for doubt,' he said, as he went to the fridge. 'Do you want anything at all?'

'No thanks.'

He came back with the can. When he opened it, beer spluttered down the side and dripped on to the carpet.

'But would she?' Joyce asked. 'You've known her longer than me.'

He shrugged. 'It looks as though she did,' he said, raising the can to his lips. 'But it's hard to imagine.' He took a drink.

Joyce wished he would use a glass. This was harder than dieting. 'Yes,' she said. 'Isn't it?'

She got up and picked up the newspaper on the pretext of intending to read it. It was open at the racing pages and she shot a quick look at Mark, but there was no point in trying to catch him unawares. She made a business of turning the paper back to the front page and sat down again.

It *was* hard to imagine. Alan had been so fastidious, so conscious of his dignity, that it was quite difficult to imagine him coping with the imperfections and absurdities of physical intimacy within marriage, never mind the furtive, hole-in-corner nature of an extra-marital relationship.

'So,' Mark said, 'it's all on again, is it?'

'Sorry?' Joyce had forgotten how the topic had been introduced in the first place.

'Frankie and Richard Hascombe.'

'Apparently.' She turned the page of the newspaper. 'It can't last,' she said gloomily. 'But I'm glad she's back.'

'I suppose they stand as much chance as the next couple,' Mark said, tipping up the beer-can to drink the dregs.

'Twenty-five years!' Joyce said. 'It's too much.'

Mark put the empty can down on the coffee table and Joyce had picked it up and taken it to the swingbin before she had time to wonder if that counted as pathological housewifery.

4

Richard came back from wherever he went after their interview, in time for Mrs Rogers's lunch, to which Frankie addressed herself with enthusiasm.

'We'll make you fat yet,' Mrs Rogers informed her as she cleared away, in her Yorkshire no-nonsense voice. 'Sweet?'

Richard had the sweet, while Frankie finished off the wine, which was dry and chilled and the perfect antidote to the warm, wet day. The small table had been set in the alcove by the french windows, but Mrs Rogers's food was more successful than her attempts at ambience, for they had barely addressed a word to one another throughout the meal.

Frankie reached out to push open the window, to hear the rain better as it fell straight and hard, hissing through the leaves. She wished she could run out in it, the lovely life-giving rain that would wash away the dust and the cobwebs through which she was walking.

Richard poured coffee and lit a cigar. The smoke drifted out of the open window and Frankie wanted to drift with it.

'Frankie – what's the matter?' he asked after a moment or two.

She finished her wine a little sadly, because she felt that perhaps she would like to get very drunk. 'Nothing at all,' she said, lifting her coffee cup as if to toast him.

Sighing, he left the table and the room and she heard his study door close. The rain had stopped without her noticing and patches of blue sky had appeared. Not quite enough to make a pair of sailor's trousers, she thought, as she went down the terrace steps and across the spongy grass to the wood. The expression was one her father had used; she felt the familiar pang of guilt.

She had to know what had happened. Alan was killed at the quarry, and almost without conscious decision that was where she was going. The pathway left Richard's garden and almost immediately twisted out of sight. She rounded the corner and could see ahead of her the summerhouse that Richard had told her about. The path forked there, running along either side of the round wooden building. She chose the left fork and hoped it would take her to the quarry. The path was narrow and the dense greenery crowded in on it; every now and then there would be consternation as some creature got out of her way.

Frankie was a town girl. She preferred the feel of paving slabs to the soft, alien earth beneath her feet. She followed the path as it weaved its way through the trees and almost broke into a run in

129

her desire to leave this claustrophobic world of animal noises and damp, rural smells, and its clinging, brushing, touching foliage.

A noise behind her made her stop. She listened, turning slowly, but there was nothing to see except the few yards of pathway behind her. Was that what Richard had heard that night? Some small animal darting through the grass? She walked on, more slowly, more quietly.

Again. She turned her head more quickly this time. She was *alone*, she told herself sternly. But she shivered, in an involuntary attempt to shake off the feeling that someone was watching her.

At last the path ran straight through the thinning wood and widened out on to the rough ground which surrounded the quarry. She could see the ragged edge, lit by a yellow, thundery light, and moved into the strange sunshine, standing for a moment to watch the shadows move quickly across the ground.

She walked to her right along the line of trees on rough stony earth which rose in an artificial mound levelling out at a vantage point on which sat a large, flat boulder, inviting her to sit down. She did so, and realised with a smile of satisfaction that she was looking at David's sketches; this was where he had sat, sketching the quarry as the sun went down.

From there she could see the other pathway, just to the right of where she sat; both paths led from the garden to the quarry. She had to talk to David. She rose and walked back down the sloping, stony ground and stood at the edge of the quarry.

It was barely a noise at all. Just the scuffing of a stone as it was unintentionally kicked. And it came from behind her.

Chapter Eleven

1

'Would you mind if I waited in the garden?' David asked.

'Of course not,' Mrs Rogers said. 'But wouldn't you rather come in and wait? Mr Rogers and I were just going to have tea.'

'Oh, thank you, but I'll wait here.' David hadn't come to brave the terrors of taking tea with strangers. He just wanted to talk to Frankie, and Hascombe had said that she was here.

'Whatever you want to do,' she said amiably. 'But it looks like rain again – just come into the kitchen when you want.'

He smiled gratefully. How did you explain to nice people that you'd sooner sit in the rain than go in and try to make conversation with them? He could never explain to anyone how shyness made him feel – they only understood it in terms of mumbling, red-faced inarticulacy. He betrayed none of these outward signs, but the mere thought of being with people he didn't know filled him with rising panic.

She went back into the kitchen, and he saw the greenhouse, just beside the kitchen door. If he pretended to be interested in the tomato plants, he'd be able just to stay there, even if it rained. He let himself into its warm depths and tried to look knowledge-ably curious, just in case she was looking.

Mr Rogers emerged from the tool-shed, locking the door, and raised his hand in greeting as he passed, as if he was always finding youths examining his hothouse plants.

Sitting down in a wicker chair, David watched the wood, because it was Mrs Rogers' belief that that was where Frankie had gone. He wondered why. He wouldn't have thought that Frankie was likely to be at one with nature.

The rain came on again, as Mrs Rogers had predicted, splattering large drops against the glass, as David kept look-out.

131

Every now and then he would get up to sniff something or read a label, but mostly he just kept his eyes on the bottom of the garden. The rain slanted through the sunshine, until it suddenly seemed to draw breath, then fell with all the force at its command.

He jumped to his feet as he saw movement, only to sit down again with a bump. Hascombe was with her. Mrs Rogers hadn't mentioned him, and now he didn't know what to do as they came towards him. He couldn't get out of his prison without their seeing him, and it was hard to know where to hide in a greenhouse.

Already drenched, they caught hands and began to run like children across the grass to the back door. Frankie was allowing herself to be pulled along as she tried to keep up with Hascombe, who ran up the steps ahead of her, opening the door. Frankie stopped dead, still holding his hand, and he let the door close again as he turned back to her. In the pouring rain, she drew him into a long, hungry kiss while David, unable to make his presence known, watched with a terrible mixture of fascination and jealousy. He turned away just as Frankie saw him and waited, a dull, sick feeling settling in the pit of his stomach. The rain was beating on the glass, the heat was almost choking him and he just wanted to die when he heard the door open. He couldn't turn round.

'What on earth are you doing in here?' she asked, her voice teasingly friendly. 'Taking up voyeurism? Because I don't think a greenhouse is quite the best cover.'

There was something about Frankie's practical approach to life that made embarrassment seem like an unnecessary luxury.

'Waiting for you,' he said, but he still had his back to her.

'You're lucky you caught me,' she said. 'I don't often come in here.'

He turned round slowly to face her. Her hair hugged her head, with tiny raindrops forming at the ends, and her eyes twinkled with undisguised amusement at his predicament.

'I wanted to see you,' he said.

'Does it have to be here?'

The wet dress clung to her, and she still looked more like a boy than a girl, David thought. She was just a skinny little redhead, and he knew he would never know anyone like her again or want anyone as much.

'I thought you'd be on your own,' he said, aware that that did not of itself explain his presence in the greenhouse.

She didn't seem to want an explanation. 'Are you coming in?' she asked.

He nodded and followed her through the mercifully empty kitchen to the sitting-room. She left him at the door.

'I have to get changed,' she said. 'I won't be a moment.' And she vanished.

David offered up a prayer to the God in which Frankie so decidedly did not believe.

'Make her say yes,' he said, under his breath. 'If You can.'

2

Frankie towelled her hair ferociously and brushed it back from her forehead.

'Is this the one?' Richard asked, producing a faded denim skirt from the wardrobe.

'If it's a skirt, then it's the one,' she said. 'I've only brought one with me.' She stepped into it and pulled a sweatshirt over her head, enjoying the feeling of the clean dry clothes as she had when she was a child and not expected to have the sense to come in out of the rain.

'Do I take it I'm forgiven?' Richard asked. 'I honestly didn't mean to frighten you.'

Frankie looked up into kind grey eyes, and couldn't believe that there had been one blood-freezing instant when she had though he might be going to kill her. She hadn't told him that; she had given vent to her feelings, but she hadn't told him that when she turned and saw him, the fear had taken a moment to turn to anger. And in that moment, she had doubted him. The kiss had been asking forgiveness, not granting it.

'Mrs Rogers said she thought that was where you'd gone – I didn't know you were just ahead of me.'

133

'I know,' she said. 'Can I ask you something?'

'Yes,' he said, a little doubtfully.

'Which path did you use that evening?' she asked.

For a moment he looked as if he might refuse to co-operate, but if he had been going to, he thought better of it. 'The one we used today,' he said. 'The low path. Should I decline further comment until I've seen my solicitor?'

She smiled. 'Sorry.' She went to the door. 'Leave it for a few moments before you come down,' she said. 'I think David wants to speak to me about something.'

And she wanted to speak to David.

3

David grew more and more nervous as he waited. He couldn't start feeling shy of Frankie, he really couldn't.

She arrived via the kitchen corridor. 'We're getting some coffee,' she said, sitting on the pouffe. 'I can't get used to this,' she said in a stage whisper. 'It's already made – I'd much sooner just do it myself.'

He smiled. 'I expect you're allowed to,' he said.

'I expect so. I don't feel as though I am.' She looked up at him. 'Come on then,' she said 'What did you want to see me about?'

The words had barely been spoken when Hascombe appeared, carrying the coffee things.

A tiny frown creased Frankie's brow and went.

'I thought I might as well bring it in,' Hascombe said, a trifle heartily.

'But David wants to talk to me,' Frankie said.

'Oh, it doesn't matter,' David said quickly. 'It'll keep.'

Hascombe put down the tray. 'Do you want me to exit tactfully?' he asked.

David wished he had never come. 'Oh, no. There's no need. It's not a secret – I just want to ask Frankie something.'

Frankie smiled. 'Go on then.'

He took a deep breath. 'I wondered if you would sit for me,' he said.

'Sit for you? I don't know, David. I might not be able to keep still enough.'

'That doesn't really matter.'

She glanced at Hascombe, then back at him. 'If you'd really like me to,' she said. 'What is it? Do you have to do a portrait or something?'

'No,' he said awkwardly. 'It's not for school. It's something of my own. It won't actually be a portrait.'

'Oh.' She grinned. 'If it's nude, you'll have to get it finished while the weather's still warm.'

'No!' he said quickly, not looking at Hascombe. 'I just want your face.'

Frankie picked up the coffee pot. 'Why the big build-up?' she asked. 'What's the catch?'

'There isn't a catch,' David said uncomfortably. 'Not really.'

She handed him his coffee. 'All right,' she said. 'I'd be delighted.'

David shifted a little. 'Well,' he said. 'You might not be.'

'What do you mean?'

Hascombe took his coffee and settled himself on the sofa, apparently taking no interest in the conversation.

'You might not like the painting. You might not understand what I'm trying to do.'

'Or I might, and that could be worse?'

David flushed. She always seemed to be able to read his mind.

Hascombe joined in for the first time. 'I'm sure Leonardo didn't ask the Mona Lisa if she *liked* it,' he said drily.

David ignored him. 'Will you still do it?' he asked Frankie

'Of course,' she said. 'But are you sure Sylvia won't mind?'

David's heart sank. He hadn't actually broached the subject with his mother.

'Of course not,' he said. 'She doesn't mind.'

4

Sylvia was setting up a picnic-style meal in the kitchen and just beginning to wonder where David was when she heard the gate to the back of the house squeak open and shut.

She smiled as he opened the back door, but there was no smile in return.

'Hello. Tea's almost ready. Have you been sketching?' She knew he couldn't have been, in view of the weather, but it was a conversation starter. Wherever he had been didn't seem to have done him much good.

'No,' he said.

It wasn't like him to be monosyllabic. 'If it's none of my business,' Sylvia said, 'I wish you would just say so.'

It would be Frankie, of course. Sylvia resolved to speak to her at the earliest opportunity. Perhaps Frankie didn't want to explain that note to the inquest, but she'd damn well explain it to her.

'It *is* your business,' David said quietly.

'What?' Sylvia was off on a different train of thought.

She could forgive Frankie a lot and had done over and over again. In the fog of half-truths and self-protection in which she had lived until the inquest, she had allowed herself to believe it all. It was easier that way. So she had believed that Frankie had bewitched Alan, as she could everyone else, because what could be more natural after all? She had believed it when she gave evidence; she had still believed it when she explained to David how it might have happened. For so indeed it might have, if Alan had been a different man. And while she had believed it, she had been prepared to forgive.

But Alan was Alan. He had not had an affair with Frankie. He had not taken his own life. That note was not a suicide note, and Frankie must know that. Twice, Sylvia had forced herself to acknowledge her real belief; once when the police had told her about Alan, and once outside the Town Hall. She had been able to reject it, to go back to the easy answer. She couldn't any more.

'What I was doing this afternoon,' David said. 'It was your business, really. I mean – it affects you.'

'Oh?' Sylvia sat down.

'I saw Frankie,' he said and looked at her from under his eyelashes, which meant he had something to confess. 'I asked her to sit for me.'

Sylvia stared at him. 'You did what?'

David ploughed on. 'She said she would if you didn't mind. Do you? Only from what you said yesterday, I thought perhaps you wouldn't. I told her you didn't.'

'What about what *you* said yesterday?' Sylvia asked.

David shrugged.

'What's that supposed to mean?' Sylvia asked sharply. 'Yesterday you seemed to think that I should be scratching her eyes out. Now you don't think I'll mind her coming here to sit for you.'

'Do you?' he asked.

'No,' she said, a little helplessly. Because she didn't, and there was very little to be gained from pretending that she did. Frankie must be a witch, she decided.

'Good,' he said, but he looked no more cheerful than he had.

'I wouldn't have thought you'd have wanted her here,' she said carefully.

'She's right,' David said. 'For the painting.'

His voice was cool and detached, and she had to remind herself that there was none of Alan in him.

If only there had been, the resemblance might not have been so chilling.

Chapter Twelve

1

Dinner had been almost like a holiday; the food, of course, had been good, but so had the company. Frankie had been entertained, made to laugh, forced to relax, with such expertise that she hadn't noticed it was happening until the brandy was beginning to take effect.

She watched Richard as Mrs Rogers cleared away, not sure that she entirely trusted someone who could press a button marked Perfect Host.

Mrs Rogers closed the corridor door.

'Why didn't you let me have five minutes with David?' Frankie asked, as soon as they were alone. It was the first reference she had made to his sudden appearance with the coffee.

He smiled apologetically. 'I thought I'd like to hear what he had to say,' he said. 'Do you think it's a good idea to sit for him?'

'I don't know,' she said carelessly. 'But I'm going to.' She kicked off her shoes and sat on the sofa, curling her bare legs under her. She wished now that she hadn't laid the subject open for discussion, since Richard had neatly turned the tables and carried the attack to her.

'You do realise how he feels about you?' Richard sat beside her.

'Of course I do.' She smiled. 'He'll get over it,' she said, her voice light.

'You shouldn't tease him,' Richard persisted.

'He expects me to.'

Richard looked concerned, and Frankie couldn't be sure whether the concern was for her or David.

'He's had a crush on me since he was ten,' she said, with what she hoped was a shrug of indifference.

'Perhaps. But he isn't ten now.'

She grinned. 'Are you jealous?'

Richard shook his head seriously. '*He* is,' he said.

The act was useless and Frankie dropped it. 'Do you think I don't know that?' she asked. 'It was David, wasn't it? It was David who believed that there was something going on between Alan and me. Wasn't it?'

Richard nodded briefly, then dismay spread over his features as he realised what she was saying. 'My God,' he said. 'You don't think that *he* killed Blake, do you?'

'I have to talk to him,' Frankie said firmly. 'And I will, when I sit for him.'

'Tell me what it is you know,' Richard said.

She shook her head. There were so many inconsistencies, so many things that didn't make sense. David's story was no less consistent than anyone else's. But she had seen the look on his face through the rain-streaked glass as he had stood watching.

'What do you want to talk to him about?' he asked.

'Practically everyone told lies,' she said. 'I think he did too.'

'What you're doing is dangerous. Supposing you do find something out? Supposing it *was* young David? What would you do then? How would you feel? What if it was Sylvia herself?'

'It wasn't Sylvia,' Frankie said.

'You don't know that,' Richard argued. 'It could have been. It really could have been.'

'Could it?' Frankie asked. 'What makes you say that?'

Richard shook his head. 'Where was she? She says she was just driving round, but you don't know that.'

'That's what she *did*,' Frankie said, 'after that sort of row. It calmed her down.'

His eyes closed for a second. 'She told the police she'd hit him back,' he said. 'I thought that was what you meant when you said someone might have told the truth. Because if it *was* the truth, then she did it after he'd left here. There wasn't a mark on him when I stopped him.'

'Then why would she say – ?' Frankie's question tailed off, as she tried to make sense of it all.

'You've thought that all along, haven't you?' she asked. 'That's what you meant when you said I'd left it too late to change my mind.'

139

He nodded briefly. 'I'm sorry I said that. It wasn't fair and I don't believe it. But when David and I went down to him, I saw the mark on his face and it wasn't bad enough to have happened when he fell.' He sighed. 'It was a silly thing to think then and it's even sillier discussing it now.'

Why would Sylvia lie? But, a little unbidden voice told Frankie, she only had Richard's word for it that she had. Richard, who had followed her to the quarry. Could the Perfect Host press another button marked Reluctant Witness? Telling her that Sylvia had lied in order to divert suspicion from himself, having shown his hand in error? But then, she argued back, Syliva *had* lied. She had lied when she said that Alan had never done anything like that before. To preserve her pride? Or her liberty?

She moved closer to Richard, in an attempt to atone for including him on her list of suspects. 'It wasn't Sylvia,' she said again. 'I just wish I could make some sense of it all.'

Richard put his arm round her. 'I'm not so sure you should,' he said.

'Can we change the subject?' she asked.

Richard took her hand. 'Yes,' he said. 'You won't like this one any better, but I've got to tell you sooner or later and it might as well be now.'

Frankie prepared herself for the blow; when it came, it almost made her laugh.

'I'm going through Blake's papers for Sylvia,' he said. 'His personal deals, the odd bit of business – you know what he was like.'

She nodded. 'What have you found? A bundle of love-letters from me?'

He smiled bleakly. 'Blake had proof, I'm afraid, that you were cheated out of quite a lot of money. About two thousand pounds. About a year ago, it seems to have been. Rainford wrote some cheques –'

Frankie let out the breath that she had been holding. 'Oh,' she said, 'it doesn't surprise me.'

'You don't sound too upset.'

'I'm not. I've been expecting it, I suppose. He loses more

140

money than he earns.' She smiled tiredly. 'He can keep it for all I care.'

Richard shook his head. 'What is it about this place? Do you intermarry or something? You're all mad! He steals from you and you say he can keep it. Blake finds out, but he doesn't tell you. Sylvia thinks you've been having an affair with her husband, but doesn't mind your popping over to have your portrait painted. You think David shoved his stepfather down a quarry and you want to *talk* to him about it – you're all mad!'

He sat up, pulling away from her.

Frankie stayed where she was, watching the back of his neck until she made him turn round.

'Mark isn't a thief,' she explained patiently. 'He would borrow it, that's all. He owes money on everything – have you seen their house?'

Richard didn't speak for a moment. 'And what are you going to do about it?' he asked.

'He can regard it as a loan,' she said and smiled suddenly. 'The repayments will be a bit erratic, horses and dogs not being the most reliable investment –'

'You can't afford to do that,' he said.

'Yes I can. I don't want that money anyway.' She shrugged. 'I'd have given him it if he'd asked. I only want him to pay it back so that he can't gamble so much.' She frowned. 'How did Alan know about it, anyway?'

Richard went over to the bureau and brought back an envelope 'Photocopies of the cheques,' he said. 'I don't know where he got them.'

Frankie looked through the pieces of paper. 'I do,' she said. 'They're from my house – this is even one of the envelopes from my writing case.' She handed them back. 'I take it that it's quite easy to see the join?'

'Oh yes. As if Rainford wanted you to see it.'

'He probably did. But I never look at the cheques or the statements. They come back from the bank and I stick them in an old shoe-box. I expect Alan was snooping around and spotted the deliberate mistake.'

Richard sat down again. 'Then why didn't he tell you?' he

asked. 'Why get them photocopied?'

Frankie raised an eyebrow.

'Would he have been blackmailing Rainford?'

This time Frankie did laugh, but Richard looked hurt, and she stopped. 'I'm sorry,' she said. 'But the idea of someone trying to blackmail Mark really is funny. How do you blackmail someone like that? He'd just pretend you weren't doing it. You said yourself he practically wanted me to find out.'

Richard nodded reluctantly.

'Mark knows that I'd never go to the police. And so did Alan, come to that.' She laughed again. 'Mark really isn't blackmail material, is he? I mean, what would you blackmail him *for*? He hasn't got a penny and the best he could manage would be a hot tip for the three o'clock at Ayr.'

At last Richard smiled too. 'It was a bit unlikely,' he said. 'But why would Blake want to keep photocopies?'

Frankie leant back. 'Just to have it,' she said. 'Just to know something about Mark. To know something I didn't know about my own money. It gave him a feeling of power, I think.' She grinned. '*That's* what turned Alan on, you know,' she said. 'Not me, I do assure you. Not women at all.'

'Not men,' Richard said, only half in fun. He looked at the envelope and took it back to the bureau.

'Not people, full stop. Property and money and position. Power. He liked to think he owned people – hitting Sylvia was like banging the telly when it doesn't work.'

'Are you serious?' Richard looked suspicious, as though expecting her to laugh at him again.

'Oh, yes. He married Sylvia because David was eight and he didn't have to put up with anything as distasteful as a pregnant woman or dirty nappies or a baby being sick on his shirt. There were certain things she was supposed to do – if she didn't do them –' She finished the sentence with a shrug.

Richard shook his head. 'A pre-packed wife and child?'

Frankie got up and took the envelope from him. 'Don't put it back,' she said.

He spread his hands. 'Tear it up, if you like,' he said. 'I don't want it.' He closed the bureau.

'Yes,' Frankie said, 'pre-packed. A convenience family.' She tore the envelope in two. 'He'd tried the real thing, but he divorced her and put his next marriage on a business footing. Because a wife is a necessary item, of course.'

Richard scratched his head and sat down on the sofa. 'Aren't you over-simplifying?' he asked. 'You make him sound like some sort of robot.'

'I suppose I am,' she said. 'But I'm not wrong. He didn't want emotional involvement – he liked to feel that he had power over people.' She sighed. 'A sort of substitute, I suppose.'

'It isn't usually a substitute,' Richard said, smiling. 'A lot of politicians would tell you that an interest in one does not rule out an interest in the other, if you'll pardon the expression.'

'It did with Alan,' Frankie said. 'I'm sure it did. I don't think he cared anything about Sylvia.'

For a moment, they sat in silence. Frankie was enjoying the moment, until Richard spoke.

'Frankie,' he said. 'What will you do if you do find out anything? Will you go to the police?'

Her fist clenched round the pieces of torn paper that she still held. 'No,' she said. They weren't the circumstances of her choosing, as she had meant them to be, but they were the best she was going to get. She twisted the pieces of paper in her hands. 'Can I tell you something?' she asked.

2

Mark padded bath-robed and barefoot from the bathroom to the bedroom and plugged in the portable TV.

'What's on?' Joyce asked.

'*Dracula*.'

He lay on the bed rather than under the one sheet that Joyce favoured during the sticky summer. He ducked his head to read the title of her book. 'Is it good?' he asked.

'Not very.' She laid it down. 'Who *is* Mrs Milray?' she asked.

Mark had thought that that moment had passed. 'What do you mean, who is she?' he asked, playing for time, but his usually agile imagination could come up with nothing but the truth.

'Who is she, that's all.' Joyce closed her book. 'She says she remembers me, and I know her from somewhere. And you know her.'

'Slightly.'

'Where did I meet her?' Joyce asked. 'I know I did.'

The film hadn't started and he couldn't pretend a deep interest in the Patagonian Welsh community at this late stage in his development. 'At Frankie's probably,' he said.

'When?'

'Well – if that was where you met her, it would probably be just after we got married.'

'No wonder I don't remember! Is she a friend of Frankie's or what?'

Mark turned up the sound on the Patagonian Welsh. 'Not really,' he said.

'What's the mystery? Who is she?'

'No mystery.'

She leant over him and turned the sound down again. 'Yes, there is. Who is she?' She kept her hand on the volume control.

Mark supposed he must have weathered this conversation rather better the first time around, but he had had too many other things to lie about in the meantime. 'I don't think she is now,' he said, 'but she was a social worker.'

Joyce left the sound turned down and knelt on the bed, facing him. 'A social worker? My God, I pity her clients – what has she to do with Frankie?'

'Frankie *was* one of her clients.'

'Frankie had a social worker?'

'She got into a spot of trouble when she was a kid,' he said. The credits were rolling on Patagonia; he reached out a hand, but it was smacked back.

'What sort of trouble?'

'Man trouble,' he said. 'What sort would Frankie have?'

'And you never told me?' she said accusingly.

'It was none of our business.' It sounded sanctimonious and was received with the derision it deserved.

144

'And I'd go shouting it from the rooftops, of course,' Joyce said, settling back on her heels, her face expectant. 'Come on – you've got to tell me now.'

He leant back on the pillow. 'I wouldn't try and speak to Frankie about it if I were you,' he said.

Joyce looked puzzled. 'Am I likely to?'

'Well – it's probably going to get dragged up again with this business,' he said. That was the awful thing. People were bound to start talking all over again. He couldn't believe that Frankie could have been so stupid, but that note seemed to say she had. Why Blake, of all people? Perhaps he was a challenge. He could imagine that appealing to Frankie.

'Are you going to tell me or do I have to tickle your feet?'

'No!' He automatically pulled his feet away from the danger area. 'All right. When Frankie was fifteen – well, just before she was fifteen, to be exact, she disappeared. And she turned up a month later living in a squat in Westbridge city centre – which would have been all right, except that the police found out that a man had been living there with her.'

It felt disloyal, even telling Joyce.

'Go on.'

'They found out who he was – he was only about nineteen himself and separated from his wife, would you believe. He'd gone off with Frankie and then he'd read a newspaper saying she was missing. So he just took off and left her there.' He watched *Dracula* flicker silently for a moment. 'They charged him, and Frankie said that he didn't know how old she was and that he hadn't corrupted her because he wasn't the first.'

Joyce looked serious. 'And was that true?'

'Who knows?' he said. 'I imagine it was. She certainly went her own way. I don't think it would have been an entirely new experience, let's say.'

'But what about him not knowing she was under age? She looks under age *now*.'

He smiled. 'I don't think he could have done or he wouldn't have been so surprised when he read the evening paper. I think she must have told him it was her sixteenth birthday coming up, and he figured it wouldn't matter.'

Joyce's brow cleared. 'Oh yes. You said it was just before her birthday.'

'That was my theory,' Mark said. 'Everyone had one, but you couldn't get any sense out of Frankie. Anyway, it got worse. Because it turned out that this joker had broken into a club in Brampton and that was why they'd run away in the first place, because the police were after him. They charged them both with the break-in, because he was seen running away from this club with someone else.'

Joyce's mouth fell open. 'That doesn't mean it was Frankie,' she said.

'They thought it did. There might have been more to it than that – I honestly don't know. But she said that she thought he wanted to get away from his wife and that she didn't know about the police being after him. Much good it did her, because they found her guilty. They went easy on her though.' He switched off *Dracula*.

'Do you think she did it?'

'No,' he said. 'I'm sure she didn't.'

'I wonder,' Joyce said.

'Anyway,' Mark said, unwilling, even now, to remember the outcome, 'you can imagine what all this was doing to Frankie's father. Court cases and social workers and police – he was hanging on by willpower as it was.'

He saw Joyce's eyes as she realised what was coming next.

'Oh no,' she said. 'Oh *no*. Poor Frankie.'

'So they started talking about putting Frankie into care,' Mark said. 'If you had seen the state she was in over her father – I think it would have finished her if they'd put her in care.'

'What happened?' Joyce got back under her sheet as a draught of air shifted the curtain for the first night in weeks.

'Sylvia fought it,' Mark said. 'And she had to fight, believe me. I couldn't have done what she did. She went to meetings and hearings and God knows what all, trying to make them see sense.'

'But I suppose Frankie was under her care when it all happened,' Joyce said. 'You can see their point.'

'Yes, I suppose so. But she argued that if Frankie had needed her before, she sure as hell needed her now. And in the end, she won.'

Joyce looked thoughtful. 'You don't really think that Frankie had an affair with Alan, do you?' she asked. 'After Sylvia had done all that?'

'I don't know,' Mark said. 'Honestly, I don't. I can't see her being that ungrateful, but what do you really know about what goes on?'

'Do you think that note was a suicide note?'

'No.' He couldn't make up his mind what he thought the note was. It could have been a note 'terminating the relationship' as Sylvia's counsel had tried unsuccessfully to suggest. But that was so hard to believe. More from Blake's point of view than Frankie's. Playing with fire was not one of Blake's hobbies – at least not with fire that he couldn't control. And Frankie was just that. A suicide note was out of the question. And that being the case, only one person could have produced it, and that was Frankie herself. All he knew was that its sudden appearance had made him feel uneasy.

'Let's hope it all dies down now,' he said. 'Frankie doesn't need all this.'

Joyce raised her eyebrows. 'Frankie?' she queried. 'What about Sylvia?'

Mark switched on *Dracula*. 'I think Sylvia's better off.'

3

'Frances,' Frankie said. 'She always calls me Frances.'

Richard had just listened; he hadn't commented, he hadn't comforted, he hadn't offered advice. He hadn't told her that her father was dying anyway and that she mustn't blame herself. Frankie had been glad of that. She had tried to tell him how the whole thing made her feel, but she didn't think she could ever explain that to anyone. 'But I didn't exactly take the veil as a result,' she finished. 'I was just more discriminating.'

'Was Blake on the scene then?' he asked, the first time he'd spoken.

'Yes, in the background. Offering my father less than his property was worth and making enough on the resale to buy the factory.'

'Oh. I don't expect he cared much for all the goings-on, did he?'

'No. He kept out of the way. They made Sylvia my legal guardian, and he didn't marry her until I was eighteen and off her hands. I don't blame him for that, though.'

Richard smiled. 'I can't say I do, either,' he said.

Frankie smiled back.

'But really!' Richard said crossly. 'Surely you and Mrs Milray don't believe that I got struck off the Old Boys' roll of honour because of that?'

'No,' Frankie said. 'That wasn't what she meant. She just wanted me to understand your reputation and tell you about mine before someone else did. In case it mattered to you.'

'How does that woman come by her information?'

'She'll have a friend with a friend. Someone has to type out the lists.'

He nodded. 'I suppose she does,' he said.

'And she knew about your daughter from the *Leader*,' Frankie said. 'There was a little article about you.'

'So she doesn't really have the house bugged?'

'I don't think so,' Frankie laughed.

'Well,' Richard said, kissing her, 'thank God for that.'

Chapter Thirteen

1

Richard woke first, while Frankie slept on. She lay half-covered, one arm flung out, the other behind her head. There was no sign in that composed, sleeping face of the terrible heart-wrenching guilt that she carried around with her. He had wished he could take it from her, store it away in his own lockable guilt compartment, to be examined from time to time during a sleepless night when his mind had nothing better to do. But the passion with which she felt the guilt was the only way Frankie could feel. Passionate guilt, passionate love, passionate anger. It might last a moment, or a lifetime; he doubted if Frankie knew herself.

The revelations of the night before hadn't entirely taken him by surprise. There was something just a little wild about Frankie, like a cat that chooses to come and live with you. You mustn't be surprised to find that she's living with the people up the road as well.

2

David paced his studio, hardly able to believe the clock. It was hours before Frankie was expected and he'd rehearsed it all a hundred times. Useless rehearsal, he knew; people didn't just hand you the appropriate feed lines.

The painting sat on the easel, waiting for Frankie, but covered so that she wouldn't see it. Sometimes, he didn't show anyone even the finished product, and he would never let anyone see his unfinished work. He didn't know if that made him less of an artist. All the ones you had ever heard of seemed to be only too pleased to be filmed working on a painting or to show the cameras round work that they were still improving; not David.

On the wall he'd pinned up the detailed, careful drawings that he'd done from his sketches. One was of a futuristic, evil aircraft, black as sin. He had to look at them, to remember what had been his original intention, before the quarry had taken on a more immediately sinister significance. Before Frankie's image had undergone a sea-change. Still – perhaps it was all grist to the mill, he thought, philosophically. Perhaps it would help.

But like a still photograph, another image of Frankie remained in his mind. A distorted image, through streaming glass, of Frankie in the rain, eagerly reaching out for Hascombe.

He'd told his mother that Frankie was right for the painting, and so she was. But that wasn't why it was so urgent to get her here.

And to get her alone.

3

'Don't you wish you'd never got involved with any of us?' Frankie asked, tentatively picking up the marmalade.

'It isn't dull,' Richard said.

'We must cover the entire range of deadly sins amongst us,' she said with a smile. 'You know mine. What's yours?'

Richard glanced across as her. 'I do know yours,' he said. 'I doubt if you do.'

'Oh?'

He pointed his fork at her. 'You're a glutton, Frankie.'

She looked at his enormous breakfast, and then at her own toast, and laughed. 'Tell that to Mrs Rogers,' she said.

'Food is about the only thing you *aren't* a glutton for,' he said seriously. 'You want more than your fair share of everything else. And you get it.'

'Do I?'

'Of course you do,' he said. 'Guilt, for instance? Love? Attention?'

Once again, Frankie did not like the turn the conversation had taken, but he wasn't going to let it go.

'What about Sylvia?' he asked. 'What did you have down for her?'

Back to Sylvia. Frankie busily spread marmalade on her toast. 'She hasn't got one,' she said stoutly.

'Avarice,' he said.

Frankie looked up. 'What? Sylvia's the most unselfish person I know!'

Richard beamed at her. 'I didn't say she was selfish,' he said patiently. 'I said she was avaricious. Which she *is*, Frankie. She married Blake to get a big house and two cars and a private education for David. She wanted an expensive lifestyle and she didn't give a damn what she had to put up with to get it.'

Frankie stared at him. It was no more than she had said to Sylvia herself; now it sounded like an accusation.

'You want me to think it could have been Sylvia,' she said. 'And you're wrong.'

'It could have been.'

'If she's so avaricious, why would she have left that note?' Frankie asked. 'She'll lose everything now.'

'Perhaps,' Richard said. 'But probably not. She'll get the insurance in the end, I'm sure. Sylvia worked in insurance – she knows that they almost always settle, even if they've got a proviso. If she did it –' he stopped. 'I said *if*,' he repeated, 'then it would be a calculated risk, like insurance itself. But I think it was an accident and nothing more.'

Frankie's anger at what seemed to be a monstrous suggestion subsided a little and she relaxed. 'I had Mark down for avarice,' she said, taking a bite of toast.

'You know that's wrong. You told me yourself last night. Mark just takes the easy way. It's easier to win money than earn it – it's easier to take it than borrow it. Easier to spend it than save it.'

'Sloth,' Frankie said and smiled. 'We really do cover them all, don't we?' She thought for a moment. 'Pride,' she said. 'Joyce?' She waited to be told that she was wrong.

'Joyce,' he agreed.

'What are we left with?' she asked. 'Anger, lust ... what's the other one?' She frowned in an effort to remember all seven at once. 'Envy,' she said proudly, then her face sobered.

'David,' she said, wishing that he would correct her and knowing that he wouldn't. She sighed. 'What did he say?' she asked. 'What did you overhear?'

'It was just after he came home from school for this holiday,' Richard said. 'I was at a sort of informal meeting at Blake's with a couple of other people who were considering investment.' He laid down his knife and fork. 'We were in the garden,' he said. 'I'd wandered off to look at his rose garden and I'd just come back. I was behind David and he didn't know it.'

Frankie felt again the panic she had felt in the wood. 'I know the feeling,' she said.

'I didn't do it on purpose that time either. Anyway, Blake was saying that he hoped they would meet you. You were his assistant and his right hand, and so on. You know the sort of thing. And David said under his breath, "I hope that's all she is." I heard him quite clearly. I don't think he even knew he'd said it.'

He carried on with his breakfast.

'Anger,' Frankie said. 'That's Alan.' She grinned. 'So that leaves you with lust.' She abandoned the toast and marmalade and poured herself coffee.

He was shaking his head again. 'Blake wasn't anger,' he said.

'What do you call what he did to Sylvia?' she asked.

'That wasn't anger. Not real anger. Sylvia was comparing you with him,' he said. 'After it happened. She said that if you lost your temper you might stick a knife in my ribs, but it would be a real knife.'

Frankie's eyes widened. 'That must have made you feel better,' she said.

'Blake's anger was manufactured. Not the real thing at all.' He tapped her hand. 'You're much too literal,' he said. 'You can lust after other things, you know.'

'So you're anger,' Frankie said, ignoring him.

'Well, I didn't go for a walk that night,' he said.

'I gathered that,' Frankie said. 'People with elaborate burglar alarms don't go off for a walk leaving their houses empty and open.'

'No,' he said. 'But before you jump to conclusions, if I'd been going to kill anyone, it would have been you.'

'Thank you.' Frankie drank her coffee.

He smiled. 'I was very angry,' he said. 'When the eyes and ears of the world left, I went diving off to talk to young David. Sylvia told me he was at the quarry. I was going to make him tell me

152

what that remark meant –' he broke off. 'I realised that I was making a monumental fool of myself and that's when it turned into a walk.'

Frankie got up from the table, and smiled. 'We could go through everyone again and you'd give us all a different deadly sin, wouldn't you?'

He laughed. 'Of course. Isn't that what the SDS are all about?'

Frankie wandered into the sitting-room, realising as she did so that she was doing something wrong.

'Oh,' Mrs Rogers said, straightening up without plugging in the Hoover. 'I'm sorry. Mr Hascombe doesn't usually use this room until later on.'

'Sorry,' Frankie said. She smiled. 'Ignore me.'

'I can do somewhere else if you like,' Mrs Rogers said.

'No. Just carry on.' Frankie was determined not to feel obliged to be where Mrs Rogers wasn't.

'I was just going to Hoover.' Mrs Rogers made it sound like an intensely private activity.

'Fine. Don't mind me.'

'I find Sunday mornings more convenient,' Mrs Rogers said, 'because the room isn't used.'

And so they stood, horns locked. No-one could ever know how important it was to Frankie that she win; she had to feel that she could make coffee when she chose, that she could go into any room she liked. Living with Richard could be easy. She wasn't so sure about living with Mrs Rogers.

'It makes a noise,' Mrs Rogers said in what Frankie recognised as a last-ditch attempt.

'Mine doesn't,' she said, with a grin. 'Is that where I'm going wrong, do you think?'

Mrs Rogers relaxed when she realised that she was not going to be watched with a critical eye and pushed home the plug.

Frankie looked round as the whine filled the room. Should she stay, now that she had won? Yes, she decided. Her eye fell on the sofa and the tiny pieces of paper into which she had shredded the envelope and its contents while she told Richard her story. She wouldn't normally have left that for someone else to clear up. Glad of something to do, she began to gather up the twisted, torn pieces, remembering her flip answer to Richard. Power. That's why Alan would want evidence of Mark's dishonesty. But to what end? She knew all too well that Alan was not above a spot of gentle blackmail, but there was nothing to be gained from having something that he could hold over Mark.

She dropped the pieces into the waste-paper basket, realising too late that it had already been emptied.

Nothing made sense. If he couldn't frighten Mark, then why keep photocopies? And no-one could frighten Mark.

Oh, but it did make sense, she realised. It did make sense.

4

Mark had just ambled downstairs and reached the phone just before Joyce did. She carried on with cooking breakfast.

After a brief conversation, Mark hung up. 'Frankie,' he said. 'She's coming to see us in about an hour.'

Joyce put down his plate. 'Do you want toast?'

'Please.' He came through to the kitchen and pulled up a stool.

Joyce flipped her egg over for a second. 'Have you told me the truth?' she asked.

'What about?' The words were indistinct, as Mark spoke through a mouthful of breakfast.

'Do you have to have the subject matter before you can answer?' She sat down. 'About this money of Frankie's. About how much you took. Have you told me the truth? Because that's what she's coming about, I'm sure.'

Mark swallowed. 'As God is my witness,' he said. 'Do we have any orange juice?'

'In the fridge. Richard Hascombe must have told her by now,' she said.

'It doesn't matter. Really, it doesn't.' He reached over and took out the carton of orange juice. 'She was always going to find out anyway. No point in worrying until she does. That might not be why she's coming – you don't know that.'

'He won't sit back and let her do nothing about it,' Joyce said.

Mark flicked open the cupboard above his head and took out two glasses. 'He can tell her until he's blue in the face,' he said. 'Nothing will make Frankie go to the police.'

Joyce took a glass. 'You're very sure of yourself,' she said miserably.

'It's Frankie I'm sure of. I told you last night – she hates the police.'

'Poor Frankie,' Joyce said and her heart grew heavier as she realised the implications. 'Oh, Mark – how could you?'

'What?' Mark had at last been surprised into a reaction. Some orange juice spilled on to the bar-top.

He really didn't know what she meant, Joyce thought. Sometimes she couldn't understand why she so much wanted to share Mark's life. 'How could you take advantage of her like that?' she asked.

'That's not true,' he protested. 'I didn't.' In a rare moment of fact-facing, he backtracked. 'All right, yes I did. But not the way you mean! I didn't think "Oh good, she's all screwed up about the cops, so I can steal money from her". I borrowed it, that's all.'

Joyce put down her knife and fork. 'Then why didn't you?' she asked. 'Why didn't you just ask to borrow it?'

'I couldn't! She – she hates even talking about that money. She thinks her father died because of what she did. That's why I do all the investment and all the work with the houses. She'd never have discussed a loan. Never.'

'So you stole it?' Joyce stared at him.

She knew that Mark couldn't explain motives he barely understood himself. Perhaps she understood it better. Emotion alarmed him – Frankie alarmed him, with her quick temper and her fierce honest reactions. Easier just to take the money first. Better than going through a Frankie three-act drama for nothing.

'You knew you could steal it because she would never go to the police,' she said.

'No! I just borrowed it without asking. She doesn't even want the bloody money!'

'Oh, I see – so you were doing her a favour, were you?' She had never been so remorselessly hard on him. 'You deliberately took advantage of her, Mark!'

'No!' he said again. 'Not of her, not of *Frankie*. Of the money – money she doesn't want to know about. Money I'll pay back. Not of Frankie.'

155

Joyce raised her eyes to heaven. 'Not of Frankie? Not of Frankie, because she might cry, or get angry, or spit in your eye? Money doesn't have feelings, so you just took advantage of it? She'd much rather you stole it?'

Mark jumped up, knocking over his stool. 'What about you?' he asked.

'Yes,' Joyce said. 'But I know what I did and I have to live with it. I don't shut it away in some attic and pretend it isn't there.'

Mark was at the door, out of sight. 'And that makes it nobler, does it? he asked bitterly. 'Does guilt make the offence any less?'

He reappeared briefly to pick up his wallet. 'I've never seen any use for it myself,' he said. 'You've either done something or you haven't. There's no bloody point in feeling guilty about it.'

And he was gone with a slamming of the door.

Joyce wiped up the orange juice.

5

Richard squinted out at the sky. 'I wonder if I'll even get nine holes in,' he said. 'It still looks thundery.'

Frankie had declined his offer to caddy for him.

'Why don't you come?' he asked again. 'You could do with some fresh air.'

She smiled. 'That air is not fresh. It's hot and sticky and I've got something else to do.'

'When are you going to sit for David?'

'Two o'clock,' she said.

'Oh – I almost forgot. I have to renew my membership today. They only let you have six months to start with in case you turn out to be a cad.'

He opened the bureau and looked through some letters. 'I've got their letter somewhere,' he said. 'I think I ought to take it with me, just in case.' His eye caught sight of a piece of paper that he had kept to show Frankie and had almost forgotten. 'Oh, by the way. You were right.'

'About what?'

'Do you remember that letter? About the ZR36/1T?' He

smiled. 'I know what it is now,' he said and picked up the sheet of paper. 'You said that Blake didn't see irate customers himself – he went off for the day and left you a memo.' He handed her the folded sheet. 'He had,' he said. 'Sylvia found it in a folder of stuff in the house.'

Frankie took it from him.

'You were wrong about one thing,' Richard said, turning back to look for the golf club letter. 'It wasn't an office equipment exhibition he'd got lined up. It was a Health and Safety one-day seminar.' He found the letter and closed the bureau.

'Anyway,' he said, turning, 'I just thought you'd like to –'

Frankie was standing with the sheet of paper in her hand, staring at him.

'What the hell?' Richard looked round, as though he might see someone else in the room. Someone who had made Frankie look like that. The ghost that she looked as though she had seen.

'Don't you see?' she said, and he really thought she was seeing ghosts.

'See what? What's the matter?'

'It just fell out,' she said, half-laughing, half-sobbing. 'It just fell out of the folder.'

The laughter was tinged with hysteria, and Richard watched helplessly. It would take a braver man than him to slap Frankie's face.

But she calmed down without his help and took a deep breath. 'There was a folder in Alan's car,' she explained slowly. 'When he was here that night. But it had gone later on. He must have taken it into the house.'

She handed him the scrawled, crossed-out, altered notes. 'Does that remind you of anything?' she asked, her voice almost a whisper, the tears not far away. '*My* note must have fallen out,' she said. 'That's all. It just fell out of the folder. It should have been with this memo.' She looked at him. 'Shouldn't it?' she asked.

Of course. That was why he had felt as though he had already seen Alan's note to Frankie.

' "This is a dreadful mess," ' Frankie quoted, her voice steadier. ' "I hope you can understand – I couldn't face starting all over again."

Richard looked at the dreadful mess that would have benefited from being started all over again, and at Frankie. Her eyes stared straight ahead of her, seeing the note as if she were holding it. She continued to recite it, word for word.

' "I know I'm running out on you, but I'm a coward and you're not. You'll get on better without me. You'll cope." ' She turned her head then to look at Richard. ' "You always do," ' she finished.

His eyes dropped from hers, from the blank defeated look. Frankie had been haunted by an elaborate apology. She had read until she knew by heart words that Alan Blake had dashed off without a second thought.

He folded the paper. 'We were all so busy reading between the lines, we forgot to read the lines themselves,' he said, handing it to her. 'I expect you'll want to keep this.'

She took it and slipped it into the back pocket of her jeans.

'So,' he said. 'No-one planted it. No-one did anything. It was an accident.'

He thought for a moment that it was the sheer anti-climax that was making her shake her head.

'No,' she said. 'It wasn't an accident. The *note* was an accident.' The light came back into her eyes. 'If there hadn't been a note, I wouldn't have suspected anything. But there was, and I did.'

Richard's shoulders sagged. For a brief instant, he'd thought it was all over. 'You're not carrying on with it, are you?' he asked. 'You can prove it had nothing to do with you now. Isn't that what you wanted to do?'

'I've got to carry on,' she said. 'I've done too much to stop now.'

Richard frowned. 'What have you done too much of?' he asked, bewildered.

'Putting two and two together.'

Chapter Fourteen

1

Frankie had forced Richard by sheer strength of will to go and play golf before the weather broke. She was walking through the cobbled courtyards of the estate, past the neat gardens, when someone matched his silent stride with hers.

'Hi,' Mark greeted her with his usual lazy smile. 'If it's me you're coming to see, the wife hasn't gone out yet.'

She smiled. 'Were you lying in wait for me?' she asked as they slowed down to a stroll.

'No. I was just out for a walk.'

They passed the industrious householders, doing it themselves with a vengeance and a power tool.

Mark laughed. 'When a future civilisation digs this place up, they'll preserve it as a shrine to the twin gods Black and Decker.'

Their steps grew slower. 'What made you come and live here?' Frankie asked, as they stopped by a wrought-iron bench.

'Joyce.' He sat down. 'I'd be just as happy in a bedsit.'

'You'd be happier,' Frankie said.

'No, not really.' He screwed his eyes up as he looked at her through sudden brilliant sunshine. 'Joyce wouldn't like it.'

Frankie sat beside him. 'Do I take it that you don't want to go home?'

He smiled. 'We had a row. But the air will have cleared by now.'

The rain began to fall softly through the shafts of greenish-yellow sunlight, sparkling down on to the low walls and ornamental stonework. In the distance, thunder began to rumble and the do-it-yourselfers began to pack up.

'We'll get caught in this if we don't hurry,' Mark said, standing up.

It irritated Frankie just a little that she was going to miss

159

another thunder storm. She loved thunder and lightning; the spectacular release of energy, the sudden violent eruption of sound, satisfied something in her. And she couldn't watch, wide-eyed and wondering, as she had as a child, unless she were on her own. She breathed in the urban smell of rain on hot pavements and smiled.

They walked briskly through the light rain to the Rainfords' house.

'Just made it,' he said, ushering her in ahead of him. 'I'll take your coat.'

Frankie wiped her shoes carefully on the mat and walked into the light, airy, open-plan room.

Joyce smiled nervously. 'Hello, Frankie – it's good to see you. It's been ages. Is that Mark with you?'

Mark came into the room. 'Why?' he asked. 'Who else has a key?'

'Wouldn't you like to know,' Joyce said with a breathless little laugh. 'I'll make some tea – Oh, no – you prefer coffee, don't you, Frankie? I'll make coffee. Is coffee all right for you, Mark? I can make both – it doesn't take a minute.'

'Either's fine for me,' Frankie said quickly, while she could get a word in. Joyce didn't usually do her thing when Mark was actually there, present and correct.

Joyce went into the kitchen, rattling cups and saucers down on to the breakfast bar, busily making whatever it was she had decided to make.

Frankie looked round at the gleaming surfaces and the self-coloured upholstery that wouldn't dare have a stain on it. The sun glinted on sparkling windows and reflected on the pale cream carpet. The carpet was three years old to Frankie's certain knowledge and still looked as though it had just been delivered. Frankie's carpets had a strong tendency to look three years old *when* they were delivered.

A scrap of paper caught her eye and automatically offended it. Her own house was knee-deep in old newspapers, envelopes with incomprehensible notes on the back, discarded packaging and unopened missives from the *Reader's Digest*, but here, she noticed scraps of paper.

And Mark, charmingly indolent, sprawled on the sofa in the

midst of the *Homes and Gardens* neatness, looked almost out of place.

Joyce was keeping up a flow of inconsequential conversation from the kitchen and Mark was glancing through the Sunday paper, discarding supplements and various sundries.

'Oh, Mark! Look what you're doing with that paper!' Joyce set the tray down on the coffee table and began to reassemble the sections, including the one that Mark had in his hands. He didn't protest.

Rain slanted against the windows. 'Mark?' Joyce said. 'Will you go up and close the bedroom windows?'

Mark went off to comply and Joyce, kneeling by the coffee table, caught Frankie's wrist. 'I won't play this cat and mouse game,' she said. 'Richard's told you what Mark did, hasn't he?'

'Yes,' Frankie said: 'He's told me.'

Joyce nodded. 'I was going to tell you. I left dozens of messages on your Ansafone thing. Mark was so sure you wouldn't tell the police. I wanted to tell you at the barbecue but that woman came. And afterwards you were so angry with someone that I couldn't. Did you ring me?' she asked. 'At about ten to nine that night?'

'Yes,' Franke said.

'I heard the phone,' Joyce confessed. 'I guessed it would be you, and I couldn't answer it. I was in the garden. Digging helps me think,' she explained. 'Any sort of hard work does. But by then I thought Mark might be wrong. That he was just saying that, just whistling in the dark. That you would tell the police.'

'But she didn't,' Mark said from the doorway, making them both jump. He smiled disarmingly as he joined them and picked up his cup. 'I'll pay it back, Frankie,' he said. 'Every penny. I'm sorry.'

'I'd rather not talk about it,' Frankie said. 'I just wanted to tell you that you can regard it as a loan. Richard will see you about paying it back. Work out with him how long you'll need.'

'We won't need long,' Joyce said. 'A couple of months.'

Frankie looked quickly at Mark; his expression hadn't changed. But the atmosphere had.

Frankie swallowed the fawn liquid that Joyce called tea in an act of true friendship and after a respectable interval took her leave of the Rainfords, declining Mark's offer of a lift back up the hill.

It was, as Joyce had said, much steeper than it looked, and though she had no need of the bench halfway up, it took her over a quarter of an hour, and she was glad to see Richard's driveway. The walk had given her an appetite for lunch and she went a long way towards making amends for her eccentric behaviour of the morning by eating most of each of the three courses.

'I'll have to go soon,' she said to Richard. 'Before he cuts his ear off.'

Richard could barely raise a smile. 'I'd rather like to see Sylvia,' he said. 'Some stuff she ought to look at – do you mind if I walk over with you?'

Frankie smiled. 'No, of course not. I'd rather like to see Sylvia too,' she said, her hand going to her back pocket for the sheet of paper, now joined by Alan's defused note. She handed them to Richard. 'But you show her these,' she said. 'It'll give you something to talk about.' She pushed back her chair.

They strolled over to the Blakes, and Richard made to walk to the front door.

'No.' Frankie caught his arm. 'We'll go round the side. David's expecting us.'

They walked round to the back of the house, where Frankie had arranged for David to let her in by the kitchen, so that she could avoid any confrontation with Sylvia before she was ready for one.

'Is that wall in a permanent state of collapse?' Richard asked.

Frankie smiled. 'That's David's wall – he rebuilds it, and it falls down. They understand one another.'

'It sounds a bit like everyone else in this neck of the woods,' Richard said.

Frankie still didn't care much for the mention of woods. The moment at the quarry came back to her, and she shivered.

'Are you all right?' Richard asked.

'Yes, of course,' she said, as they pushed open the gate to the back entrance.

David let them in and Frankie followed him straight through the kitchen to the back stairs.

David showed her into his studio. 'I just want to draw today,' he said.

162

'Fine,' she said. She hadn't seen the studio before; they had spared no expense. The despised Alan had had his uses, she thought. 'This is lovely, isn't it?' she said, looking at the panoramic view of the valley. 'I hope the storm comes. I'll bet it would look good from here.'

She turned to the opposite wall and the pinboard with the sketches of the quarry and of the plane.

'Am I in the same picture as the quarry?' she asked. 'Is that what you thought I might not like?' She turned to face him.

'Partly,' he said. 'Does it bother you? I had it all planned before – I mean, that's why I was there.'

It did, a little. But she decided that it would hardly affect her. It wasn't even a portrait. She was just a character in a painting.

'Not really,' she said, sitting in the armchair that David indicated.

'If you're not comfortable, just say so,' he said. 'And if you want to stretch your legs or – anything, just tell me.'

'Right.' She immediately felt her features freezing.

David picked up his sketch pad. 'Just relax,' he said. 'You can talk – all I want you to do just now is look at the furthest thing you can see over my right shoulder, out of the window.' He turned the pages of the pad. 'Providing it's going to stay there,' he added with a smile. 'Don't pick a mobile shop.'

There had been a distinct shift in relationships now that she was on his territory; here, he was in command of himself and she was the artist's model, holding as much sway as a bowl of fruit. She found a telegraph pole and stared at it.

'Don't peer,' he said, his pencil moving all the time. 'If it's too far away to look at comfortably, choose something closer.'

Frankie found something closer.

'That's lovely,' he said. 'Now – that's your point of reference. Each time you sit, get really comfortable in the chair and when I need you to, I'll ask you to look at whatever it is. What is it, by the way?'

Frankie let her eyes rest on him. 'Richard's driveway,' she said.

'Oh,' he said, tight-lipped. He worked for a moment or two without speaking.

She smiled encouragingly. 'David?' she asked. 'What did you want to see me about that night? You said you came to ask me something.'

'This,' he said promptly. 'I wanted to ask you to do this.' He glanced up at her. 'Could you look at your landmark?' he asked.

Your landmark. She looked at her landmark. Just a sweep of gravel and the edge of a lawn, and it felt like home. She wondered if it was.

2

Sylvia put the two sheets of paper side by side on the table. Sheets of the same pad, each with a tiny piece missing from the corner, because they had been torn off together. Written with the same pen.

'I owe Frankie an apology,' she said. She turned away from them and sat opposite Richard.

'She doesn't think you really believed that she was involved with Alan,' he said. 'Did you?'

'You know I didn't,' Sylvia said. 'But you convinced me that it was possible. I don't believe it now.'

Richard took out a packet of cigars and undid the cellophane. 'She –' he paused. 'I didn't really want to tell you this,' he said. 'She's convinced that someone actually killed Alan.'

Sylvia didn't know how Richard had expected her to receive his statement and she assumed that her answer would surprise him. 'Someone did,' she said.

But he barely reacted at all. A slight confirmatory nod. 'She thought that someone had planted that note,' he said.

Syliva looked over at the table. 'Did she?' she said. 'That must really have bewildered her.'

But Richard didn't seem to hear what she was saying. 'I wish she'd drop it now,' he said.

Sylvia rose. 'I'm sure she will,' she replied, picking up the sheets of paper and folding them together. She gave them back to him.

'She says she's carrying on,' he said, his voice urgent. He put the notes in his jacket pocket.

Sylvia gave him a pat on the shoulder. 'Well, she would, wouldn't she?' she said.

He looked up sharply. 'What do you mean?'

Sylvia dissembled slightly. 'That's Frankie,' she said. 'She's fond of centre stage – you can't have got off so lightly that you haven't noticed.' She sat down again.

'I think you're being a bit hard on her,' he said, springing to her defence. 'She's had a bad time, you know.'

'So have I,' Sylvia reminded him. She leant forward. 'Richard – I love Frankie. As much as you do. I've known her for almost sixteen years, and I still love her.' She smiled briefly. 'It remains to be seen whether *you* can say that in sixteen years,' she said. 'But everything *about* her is dramatic. Her actions are dramatic, her emotions are dramatic – her weight loss is dramatic, for God's sake.' She sighed. 'I have to be hard on her or I begin to believe it.'

Richard shook his head. 'Why shouldn't you believe it?' he asked. 'The weight loss is real enough.' He was searching his pockets for matches.

She nodded tiredly. 'But what else is? She *wanted* us to believe that she and Alan had had an affair.'

Richard began to argue, but Sylvia held up a hand. 'I know, I know. She denied it. But she knew we would have to believe it if she said that it was a suicide note. Perhaps providence provided the note and perhaps it didn't. But Frankie wanted us to fall for it.'

'You didn't see her yesterday,' he said.

'No,' Sylvia agreed. 'But it's all right. I'll catch the second house.'

Richard was shocked. 'That isn't fair,' he said.

'Isn't it?' Sylvia pushed the table-lighter towards him. 'The coroner didn't see her yesterday, either. And there's nothing so convincing as Frankie telling the truth.'

Richard lit his cigar, and Sylvia could see that he knew what she meant.

'She's tightrope walking,' she told him. 'And I'm going to find out why. That means I have to remind myself that she isn't made of glass. If you call that unfair, or being hard on her, then that's what I'm going to be.'

Richard inhaled smoke and expelled it. 'She isn't the only one who's tightrope walking,' he said. 'Is she?'

No, Sylvia thought. Frankie had got them all doing it. And it was going to stop.

3

She didn't look well, David thought. Half of him was worried for her, as he looked at the thin shoulders and the too-sharp collar bones. And half of him knew that that was exactly how she should look. The suggestion of shadow under the clear, clear eyes. The skin, pale and slightly freckled, taut over her cheekbones. Young, fresh, unlined skin whose colour would return. A strained, tired face that would triumph over the weariness, because the vitality was all there, in her eyes.

But he wished, as he worked, that it wasn't Frankie he was itemising so dispassionately. He wished he could tell her not to drive herself so hard. She didn't speak; she sat as motionless as the drawing itself and she had forgotten he was there.

Suddenly, the light was gone, as though someone had switched off the sun. He looked up to see a thunder cloud hanging like a threat over the valley. 'Here's your storm coming,' he said, laying down the pad.

'Do you mind if we hang on?' she asked. 'I'd like to see it.'

David rubbed his eyes. 'Of course not,' he said.

Frankie stretched and massaged her neck. 'I'm sorry,' she said. 'I've not been very good company.'

She was looking at the quarry sketches again, her back to him. She turned suddenly. 'Can I see what you've just done?' she asked.

He wanted to refuse. But it was only a sketch, and he couldn't plead tradition. She knew she wouldn't see the painting, but sketches were different. He reached over to the desk and reluctantly opened the sketch pad at the appropriate page. He handed it to her.

She smiled a thank you and turned her attention to the drawing, her face growing serious. She looked up at him. 'I'm not as thin as that, am I?'

'Yes.' There wasn't much point in being chivalrous. He'd drawn it, after all.

166

She handed it back, her eyes troubled.

'Why are you letting him do this to you?' he asked, closing the pad again.

'Who?' she snapped suddenly.

'Blake, of course!' He realised that he had been thoughtless and softened his tones. 'I'm sorry,' he said. 'You liked him better than I did.'

'But not as much as you seem to have thought,' she said.

David felt his face grow hot. 'Are you still angry about that?' he asked.

'You asked me why everyone believed it,' she said. 'Do you remember?'

'Yes.'

'Shall I tell you why?'

She was going to, whether he wanted her to or not, he could tell.

'Because you jumped to conclusions,' she said. 'And you made a remark that Richard overheard. So then he believed it. And then Alan died, and this note turned up. We know what it is now, by the way,' she said. 'But you know what it sounded like. And Richard was already convinced, so Sylvia began to believe it too. And that was all because of you, David.'

David licked his lips, which had gone dry as he listened. 'I'm sorry,' he said. He put the pad back on to the desk. 'But that wasn't what I meant. Just now, I mean. You *did* like him better than I did.'

Her eyes fell slightly. 'Maybe I did,' she said. 'But it wouldn't be hard, would it?' Her voice was flat. 'I just knew where I was with him, that's all. Which is more than I can say for anyone else.'

It was now or never. 'Like Hascombe?' he said.

She looked at him for a long time. 'Don't,' she said, moving to the window, looking out at the gathering storm.

'You're not serious about him,' he said. 'You can't be.' It was obvious to everyone who knew Frankie that she was.

Behind her, the sky grew darker, with trails of smoke-grey cloud moving across it.

'He wants me to marry him,' she said, after some deliberation, and she turned from the window to look at him.

167

David's heart felt like lead. 'You haven't said yes. You haven't, have you?'

Now, the colour began to flare in her cheeks. At least it was a reaction. 'Why not?'

'He's too old for you,' David said desperately.

Before she could answer, he shouted his prepared statistic. 'When you're Mum's age, he'll be seventy!'

Lightning forked across her gun-metal grey backdrop.

'Seventy,' he repeated, because the shot had gone home.

4

Thunder, muted and lazy, rolled round the valley.

Sylvia lit the table lamps. 'I think they'll stay up there,' she said. 'I think Frankie will want to watch the storm.' She sat down and smiled sympathetically at Richard. 'She will get over this, you know,' she said. 'Whatever happens.'

Richard raised an eyebrow. 'I said she was a survivor once,' he murmured. 'I hope I was right. She's going to find things she isn't looking for.'

Sylvia watched him light his second cigar. 'If she insists on leaving no stone unturned,' she said, 'she's going to see what's underneath them, whether she wants to or not.'

5

The room swiftly darkened, as the thunderclouds massed. David had scored a direct hit and seemed intensely miserable about it.

Lightning lit them for a second, accentuating the gloom.

'Don't you see?' he said. 'It's wrong.'

Frankie shook her head. 'It doesn't feel wrong,' she said.

The thunder crashed above their heads and died away, grumbling. Frankie could hear the rain battering the glass behind her. And slowly her spirit reasserted itself.

'What gives you the right to decide what's right and wrong?' she asked sharply.

David's brown eyes looked away from hers. 'Nothing,' he said.

'But you mustn't marry him.' Thunder rumbled as he spoke.

'What is this, David?' she asked. 'Jealousy?'

He looked back at her, truly startled. 'What?' he said. 'No! No – I mean–' He searched for appropriate words. 'I won't pretend I don't –' He floundered. 'But I'm not *simple*, Frankie!' he finished.

It broke the tension for just a moment, and they smiled at one another.

But David's face grew serious again. 'But not him, Frankie. Please. Listen to me.'

'Why?' She had to go on, now that it had got this far.

The room blinked white and thunder exploded and echoed.

'Why?' she asked again, advancing on him.

He backed off slightly. 'You don't know him well enough,' he said. 'You don't know him at all. How do you know you can trust him?'

Frankie stopped. 'What does that mean?'

David looked hunted.

'Tell me what you mean,' she demanded as lightning sizzled through the air.

'He lied,' David said. 'That night. I don't know where he was, but he didn't pass me in the wood!' The end of the sentence was shouted over the peal of thunder that seemed to rattle the glass.

'Because you weren't there,' Frankie said.

'I was there,' he said hotly. 'But he wasn't, Frankie – not when he says he was.'

Frankie had been waiting for this all along and now she didn't know how to cope with it.

'He said he'd heard me in the wood,' David said. 'About five hundred yards from the quarry.' He closed his eyes as lightning flashed. 'If he did, then he was at the quarry *during* the barbecue, not after it.' The thunder, rumbling, rolling, bumping, punctuated his speech. 'Because the party was still going on when I got to Hascombe's,' he said.

Frankie went cold. 'What are you trying to do?' she asked.

6

Mark sat on his own in the living-room, still just how it was when Frankie had left.

The inevitable row had broken as soon as she'd gone; Frankie couldn't ever keep her reactions to herself. It had ended with Joyce running upstairs in tears, and there she'd stayed ever since.

And he'd stayed where he was, because he had to think, and it wasn't something he was used to. But now, he had come to a conclusion. He walked slowly to the stairs.

'Joyce,' he called quietly.

7

David could see how angry she was, angry and hurt. But he had had to tell her.

'I don't know what he was really doing,' he said. 'I'm not saying that. Just that he wasn't where he says he was.' He swallowed nervously.

Frankie shook her head, her green eyes coldly and steadily keeping him prisoner.

'It's true,' he insisted.

Again, the shake of her head. But at last she looked away as her eye went to his sketches.

His whole body went limp; he put his hands on the desk to steady himself. He knew what he was telling Frankie. Hascombe had used him for an alibi, sounding as though he was confirming David's story when in fact he was establishing his own – that's what he was telling her.

The image of Frankie in the rain floated into his mind as he watched her rip something from the board. He had to make her believe him. He had to.

She thrust the drawing under his nose, and he saw his fighter.

'When did you do that?' she demanded.

Thunder grumbled round the sky.

'That night,' he said, bewildered by the question.

'Why?' she demanded to know.

'What? Frankie – what's this about?'

The thunder whimpered in the distance.

'What made you draw an aeroplane?' she asked. Her voice was quiet, but she was shaking with tension.

'A jet came over very low. I started sketching it.' He shrugged. 'That was when I knew what I wanted to paint,' he added. 'And I wanted to ask you straight away. That was when I went to Hascombe's.'

But she was shaking her head again. 'That's not true,' she said.

'But it is! It *is*,' he repeated. It was all he could do.

'That plane and the one later when we were all in Richard's house were one and the same,' Frankie said. 'It was the only one out on exercise that night.' She threw the drawing on to the desk. 'And I know where almost everyone was when it came over the first time.'

'I don't see –'

'Shall I tell you?' Her voice was sharp, cutting through his protest. 'Alan was here, on the phone to me. I was at home. Joyce was in the garden and Mark was just knocking at his own front door. Richard was saying goodnight to Mrs Milray, who was the last to leave the barbecue.'

David couldn't see immediately where her proof lay.

'And you were drawing at the quarry,' she said. 'If you *had* left then to come to see me, then you'd have found an empty garden, like Mark did.' She took a breath. 'Wouldn't you?'

'The barbecue was still going on,' David said helplessly. 'I *did* leave then. And it was still going on when I got there, whatever time your precious plane came over!'

Frankie turned away. 'For God's sake, David!' She faced him again. 'Which are you going for?' she asked. 'Timeslip? Or are Mark and Mrs Milray and Richard in a conspiracy?'

David would believe anything. 'I don't know,' he said. 'All I know is that the party was still going on and that's why I didn't come any further, because I got nervous.'

'What do you mean, further?' Frankie asked suddenly. 'You said you were in Richard's garden.'

'I was. I was at his summerhouse.'

The wind was temporarily removed from Frankie's sails, for which David was very thankful. But she wasn't becalmed for long.

'But you can't *see* his garden from the summerhouse! You can't see the lawn – that's where the barbecue was. So how could you know it was still going on? You couldn't see it!'

'I could *hear* it! I heard the music, so I turned back.'

Frankie grasped his shoulders. 'But it was *over*,' she said, trying to shake him. 'It was over.'

'I don't care. I heard the music. It was when I heard the music that I got scared and went back. I can even tell you what it was! It was the *Deer Hunter* music.'

The ineffectual shaking stopped and her grip suddenly relaxed. 'The tape. . .' she said, and tailed off. Her hands were still on his arms, as she thought something through. 'It was the tape,' she said softly, speaking to herself.

'David? There are two paths from the quarry, aren't there? Which one did you use when you came here?'

'The high path,' David said. 'I sketch up at the top, and the high path's nearer.'

She nodded slowly. Her eyes searched his, and there were tears in them. 'David, I'm so sorry.'

He had almost to catch her as she leant against him, and he discovered that he had his arms round Frankie O'Brien.

'You thought I did it?' That possibility hadn't occurred to him.

She looked up at him. 'David, I'm sorry,' she said.

He smiled. 'Crazed by jealousy?' he asked.

'No,' she said. 'No. I never thought that.' She relaxed. 'You're making fun of me,' she said.

'You make fun of me.' He kissed her. A gentle friendly kiss. He kissed Frankie O'Brien.

'I was so afraid it was you,' she said.

David suddenly became aware of what had been happening. 'Is that why you let them think it was suicide?' he asked, his voice just a whisper. 'Because of me?'

Frankie shrugged a reply. 'Come on,' she said. 'We'll have to go down.'

She opened the door and went out ahead of him.

'Frankie,' he said softly as she started downstairs.

She turned, looking up at him.

'I won't always be sixteen,' he said.

Chapter Fifteen

1

Richard was on his own when David and Frankie came into the room.

'I don't suppose you got much work done,' he said to David.

'I'd finished, really,' he said. 'I was just doing a sketch today.'

Surprised by the length of David's utterance, Richard looked quickly at Frankie, who winked from behind David's back.

'Sylvia's on the phone,' Richard said, trying not to look as though he had been winked at.

'Is she?' David nodded, smiling at him.

Frankie was half-sitting, half-leaning on the sideboard. David sat down on the window seat.

'You didn't miss this one,' Richard said to Frankie, feeling a little as though he were talking to a stranger.

Her face went into an attitude of polite enquiry.

'Thunderstorm,' he explained. 'You didn't miss this one.'

'No,' she said, smiling too much, as if he didn't speak the language.

Sylvia came back. 'That was –' she broke off as she saw Frankie.

Frankie pushed herself away from the sideboard and ran into Sylvia's arms.

Richard felt as though he'd turned over two pages at once, as Sylvia hugged Frankie, patting her like a baby, her hard words forgotten. She stood back a little, holding Frankie's hands in hers, as Frankie blinked away tears.

'Oh, Frankie,' she said.

'Stop saying "Oh, Frankie". You're wrong. You are.'

Somehow, this seemed to constitute a conversation, thought Richard. Frankie and David were right to nod and smile at him. Clearly, he didn't speak the language at all.

'Is there any chance of my knowing what you're talking about?' he asked.

Frankie nodded. 'Sylvia thinks I killed Alan,' she said airily. 'I knew what that "Oh, Frankie" meant outside the Town Hall. Sylvia thinks it was me. I don't know why.'

Richard and David both stared at Sylvia, who still had Frankie's hands. 'I'll tell you why,' she said to Frankie. 'Alan made you very angry that night, didn't he?'

'Oh.' Frankie flushed slightly. 'You overheard that, did you?'

Sylvia nodded. 'That's what our row was about,' she said.

Frankie's face fell. 'That happened because of me?' she said.

'Yes,' Sylvia replied.

Frankie pulled away and walked over to where Richard sat.

'I didn't know that,' she said, sitting down with a bump on the arm of his chair. She looked back at Sylvia. 'I'm not worth getting beaten up for.'

Sylvia sat down. 'I think you are,' she said.

The bravado was gone and Sylvia was in charge. Richard took Frankie's hand, and squeezed it. 'What did he say to you?' he asked.

Frankie didn't look at him. 'He reminded me about my colourful past. His phrase.'

'Why? Why would he drag that up?'

'He was angry at me,' she said. 'He thought I must have influenced you about the money. If you listened to my opinion of him, he would give you his opinion of me – that sort of thing. He suggested that I try to change your mind first.'

And then Mrs Milray had come along and reinforced it all. No wonder Frankie had fled. Richard held her hand tighter.

'You were at the quarry when I got there,' Sylvia said. 'You knew there was something wrong, Frankie.'

'Not because I made it happen.'

'And then the note appeared. And you set about making everyone believe it.'

David tried to speak, but Sylvia wasn't brooking interruptions. 'You wouldn't speak to anyone before the inquest,' she said. 'And it worked, Frankie. I made myself believe it. Because it was easier that way.'

Frankie didn't look at anyone.

'Just after the inquest, I came to my senses, but I pushed it away again. I can't any more, Frankie. Alan didn't commit suicide. And you were as likely to be having an affair with the man in the moon as you were with Alan.' She looked at Richard, signalling a quick apology for what she was about to do.

'And yesterday,' she said, 'You made sure Richard stopped believing it, because it had served its purpose.'

Richard looked away from the reproachful look.

'That's why I was afraid. I thought you'd lost your temper and hit him, and he'd fallen into the quarry. I didn't understand what you were doing there, that was all. But that's why I told the police that I hit Alan back. I didn't hit him back, Frankie.'

'I know,' Frankie said.

'If I didn't,' Sylvia said, 'who did?' She paused. 'And why the charade?'

David jumped up. 'She thought it was *me*,' he said. 'That's why. Leave her alone!'

Sylvia glanced dispassionately in his direction and he left the room, slamming the door. She returned her direct brown gaze to Frankie. 'Did you?' she asked in tones of polite interest.

'Yes,' Frankie said. 'But I was wrong.'

'So you put yourself through all this for nothing?'

Richard could feel Frankie tense up. 'Nothing?' she asked. 'What was Alan doing at the quarry? And who was with him?'

'Why do you think someone was with him?' Richard asked.

Frankie was holding his hand as tightly as a child when she answered. 'Because the passenger door was unlocked,' she said, still looking at Sylvia. 'When I went for the torch, it was unlocked. And it had been locked before. So he must have had a passenger.'

Sylvia shook her head in exasperation. 'Could we dispense with the melodrama, Frankie? Of course it doesn't mean he must have had a passenger!'

'I can't think of any reason he'd unlock his passenger door unless he wanted to open it,' Frankie said, her voice so quiet that even Richard had to strain to hear. 'And I can't think why he'd want to open it to drive up to the quarry. I can't think why he'd want to drive to the quarry at all, especially when he'd been drinking. I can't think how he'd get a bruise on his face in the process.'

A muscle worked in Sylvia's face as she composed her reply.

'And I'll tell you what I can't believe,' she said. 'I can't believe that someone persuaded Alan to drive them to the quarry in order to hit him or push him over or anything else. On what pretext? Why would he go with them? He was alone in the house – if someone wanted to see him alone, why the quarry?' She took a deep breath. 'Unless, of course,' she said, carefully measuring her words, 'it was someone with a heightened sense of drama.'

Frankie's hand slipped from Richard's, as she turned to him. 'Would you mind going up to see David or something?' she asked. 'I'd like to speak to Sylvia.'

Richard looked across at Sylvia, then back to Frankie, and he really didn't know whom he would back to win.

2

The evening sun shone softly in a sky hazed with high cloud, now that the storm had passed.

Joyce sat on the patio, watching the forget-me-nots move in the gentle breeze. They should have been taken out; they were nearly all dying. The lawn had clumps of clover in it; the grass should really have been cut yesterday. If Mark had used the lawn dressing that she'd bought, it wouldn't have all that clover. And the bee that moved tirelessly from flower to flower, from clump to clump, would have had to go elsewhere. There was a break in the edge of the lawn; she'd meant to do a repair, but she hadn't. She looked at the bit she'd dug up that night, in her spot of therapeutic gardening. She hadn't planted anything, and weeds were growing now.

She hadn't Hoovered today. She hadn't even made the bed. The teacups sat where they had left them on the coffee table. She hadn't had lunch; she wondered if Mark had.

3

'Why were you at the quarry?' Sylvia had waited until the door was closed before asking.

Frankie's eyes slid slowly round towards her. 'I told you at the time,' she said. 'I thought Alan had done something awful.'

So she had. And Sylvia remembered that she had been impatient with her. 'Why did you think that?'

'He was drunk,' Frankie said. 'That meant he'd hit you. I'd had a row with Richard and I was coming back to see him when I saw Alan's car.' She looked at Sylvia, her eyes earnestly wide. 'You know what he was like about driving,' she said. 'He wouldn't have got into the car if he'd had a Tia Maria, never mind half a bottle of Scotch.'

Sylvia nodded. That had been her first thought; somehow it had got lost in amongst everything else.

'So I thought that whatever had happened, had happened *there*.' Her eyes dropped again. 'And I thought it had happened to you,' she said. 'And that you'd run away from him, and he'd gone and got drunk and rung me up looking for you.'

Sylvia felt a pang when she thought of Frankie, running to meet her car, when she had been so irritable with her. She firmly put it out of her mind. One of them had to remain rational, and it wouldn't be Frankie.

'What made you think it was David?' she asked.

'It doesn't matter,' Frankie said. 'I just did.' She stood up. 'Can I have a drink?'

Sylvia waved a hand towards the sideboard. Frankie removed the stopper from the decanter. It slipped from her hand, rattling against the tray and bouncing off to roll under a chair, and she knelt down to retreive it.

'I'll pour it,' Sylvia said, going over to her. She poured a large brandy, but Frankie didn't pick it up. She just perched on the sideboard as she had before, turning the glass stopper over and over in her fingers.

Sylvia watched her, trying to get inside her head, as she had so often done before. Frankie's motives were sometimes obscure.

'Why did you think it was David?' she asked again.

Frankie rolled the stopper between her palms. 'I saw David's sketch pad that night,' she said. 'He'd sketched a plane that had buzzed the village. I'd heard it when Alan rang me.' She affected a deep interest in the stopper.

'Go on,' said Sylvia.

'Everyone remembered that plane,' Frankie said. 'Richard's party was over by the time it appeared.'

Sylvia frowned. 'What's wrong with that?'

'Nothing, as it turns out,' Frankie said. 'But if David *had* seen the party still going on, and been back at the quarry when the plane came over, then he must have been there when Alan was.' She spun the stopper on the tray, then picked it up. 'I thought that was what he'd done. I thought he'd come to the barbecue, seen Alan hit you, and –' She didn't finish the sentence. 'And then the note turned up,' she said. 'I didn't know what to make of it.'

'So you used it,' Sylvia said.

'I told the truth!' Frankie held the stopper between forefinger and thumb and let it catch the sunlight. 'It was up to other people to think what they liked.'

Frankie had taken everyone on to protect David. 'But didn't you think about what it would mean?' Sylvia asked.

A shake of the head. 'I didn't care.'

'But you did, Frankie. You told Richard you cared about what everyone thought.'

Frankie's head shot up. 'He has no business talking about me!' she shouted.

Sylvia tried to defuse the situation by picking up Frankie's glass. 'I thought you wanted a drink,' she said.

'Not yet.' She passed the stopper from hand to hand. 'I *wouldn't* have cared,' she said. 'But after the inquest, you said "Oh, Frankie", and I knew what you thought.'

She let the stopper drop a little way and caught it. 'And I wondered if I was doing the same to David.'

'And you were?'

'Yes.' The stopper was thrown into the air a few inches and caught.

Sylvia let her do it twice more before it got too much for her.

178

She neatly fielded it, putting it firmly back into the decanter.

Frankie, deprived of her comforter, picked up her brandy and gently rocked it to and fro in the glass. 'I just wanted to speak to David,' she said. 'I didn't want this. I didn't want to start wondering about everyone.'

'Frankie.' Sylvia put out her hand to stop the movement of Frankie's glass. 'Do you know who it was?'

Frankie stared into the brandy.

'Do you?' Sylvia repeated.

'I think I've probably known all along,' Frankie said.

4

David glanced up at Hascombe as he sketched. Hascombe was staring out of the window, lost in thoughts that David could guess at. Because they weren't so very different, he imagined, from his own. Despite the thirty-five-year gap. Was it easier, he wondered, to bridge a generation than it was a decade? For the first time, he began to understand that it might be the same for Frankie, and the liaison didn't seem so unlikely after all.

'There you are,' he said a little shyly, sliding off his stool and handing Hascombe the sketch. It was a caricature, really, of Hascombe worrying.

Hascombe laughed. 'Can I keep it?'

'Of course you can.' He hadn't been sure how Hascombe would react, but it was in its way a peace offering.

He had been far from pleased to discover Hascombe at his studio door, seeking asylum. He had wanted to be on his own, to work on his painting. He'd had to rush to remove it from public gaze, and it had to be Hascombe of all people. But as he had before, David had found himself enjoying Hascombe's company, simply because Hascombe seemed to enjoy his.

'Do I look that bad?' Hascombe was asking, in fun. He reminded David of Frankie asking if she really was that thin. She'd been worrying about him, all this time. He just smiled and put his pencil away in the jar that Frankie had given him last birthday.

'What line do you think you'll take up?' Hascombe asked.

'Graphics – that sort of thing?'

Van Gogh hadn't done graphics, that sort of thing. David made a noncommital noise. 'Do you know why Frankie wanted you to leave?' he asked.

Hascombe took out his cigars. 'I think she's worked out what happened to your stepfather.'

David closed his eyes. 'Does it really matter?' he asked. 'He's dead. It won't alter that.'

'I suppose not,' Hascombe said, then suddenly grinned. 'It's all right for you,' he said, searching for matches. 'You'll be pleased to hear that you've been exonerated.'

David laughed. 'Considering that we're stuck up here together, I'd have said that was all right for *you*.'

5

'I was the only one who knew that Alan had got drunk that night,' Frankie said. 'Everyone else only knew because I told them. Except one.' Frankie took her brandy over to the sofa and sat on the floor, curled up like an underfed cat.

'Who?' Sylvia sat down, with Frankie at her feet.

Frankie shook her head. Sylvia touched her shoulder. 'Don't I have a right to know?'

'I don't know,' Frankie said, sniffing away tears. 'I don't know.' She turned her head away.

'Frankie.' Sylvia made her look at her. 'Are you saying that this person had a right to kill Alan?'

'No! But it wasn't *like* that. I'm sure it wasn't like that! Let me explain – let me tell you what I know. I might have got it wrong.' She turned away again, her hair falling over her face.

Sylvia patted her. 'All right,' she said.

Frankie looked up, her face streaked with tears that she had tried to wipe away. 'Don't make me tell the police,' she pleaded.

How could she give that sort of guarantee? 'We'll see,' Sylvia said. We'll see. *Can I have a bicycle?* We'll see. *Can I go to a party in Westbridge?* We'll see. *Can I let someone get away with killing Alan?* We'll see.

'About a year ago, Mark took some money from me,' Frankie

180

said. 'He did something not very clever with some cheques, I think.'

Sylvia groaned. 'Oh no. I didn't think he'd got that bad.'

Just for a moment, the spark returned to Frankie's eye. 'Richard doesn't tell you all my business, then?' she said. But the spirit died at birth. 'Alan had photographs of the cheques,' she said, slumping back down.

Sylvia wasn't surprised. Alan had liked to have knowledge, knowledge that he could use if he wanted to, or needed to. That was what he'd been doing to Frankie that night. But Mark? It was hard to see what capital there was to be made from holding anything over Mark.

'But what was the point?' she asked. 'You would never do anything about it.' She stroked Frankie's hair back from her face. 'And Mark would know that. That's why he was brave enough to do it, I suppose.'

Frankie nodded. 'He couldn't frighten Mark with it,' she said. 'And if he could have, there would have been no point. But he could frighten Joyce, and I think he did.'

'Joyce?' Sylvia looked blank.

'Inside information. She works for Westbridge City Council, and Alan made some very shrewd moves for someone who had let two businesses go bust.'

Sylvia made Frankie look at her. 'Do you *know* that's what he did?'

'It depends what you mean by know. I wasn't there when he did it. But I went to see Joyce today, and she asked if Richard had told me about what Mark had done.'

Sylvia frowned. 'What's Richard got to do with it?'

'Nothing. Except that he *did* tell me. Because he's going through Alan's papers for you. Joyce knew that, and what he'd find there. She *knew* that Alan had evidence. So Alan must have told her.' She sighed. 'She was so afraid that I'd tell the police,' she said, her eyes filling with tears. 'Alan made her think that I would. Until she finally told Mark what was going on and then she tried to get hold of me. I just wish she'd done that in the first place,' she said, laying her head on Sylvia's knee.

'But you can't think that Joyce *killed* Alan,' Sylvia said. 'If she did give him information, it was to hang on to her house and her garden and Mark – probably in that order. She would never endanger that – she would never have *killed* him, Frankie.'

'But he wasn't killed on purpose! Someone hit him. And he fell.'

Sylvia shook her head. 'If it wasn't on purpose, why was he at the quarry? Someone must have got him there somehow. You can't have it both ways.'

'I can. I don't think he *went* to the quarry. I think he was taken, because he was already dead.'

Sylvia stared. 'What?'

'They said he struck his head on quarry stone. He didn't have to be at the quarry to do that, did he? That's what David's wall's made of. And something knocked it over.'

'They'd know that,' Sylvia argued. 'They'd know if he'd been moved.'

Frankie shrugged. 'They might. But not if they weren't looking. And they thought they'd found a suicide note from the word go.' She took Sylvia's hands. 'It's the only way it could have happened,' she said. 'He was drunk and he was waiting for you – he wasn't suddenly going to take it into his head to go to the quarry the moment he hung up the phone. Someone came here and hit him. He fell and hit his head. When they realised he was dead, they took him to the quarry to make it look as if he'd fallen there. They used his car, left it there and came back through the wood.

'It had to be that way,' she said, her face glistening with tears of which she was quite unaware. 'It had to be that way. There wasn't time for anything else.'

'Joyce?' Sylvia asked. 'Was it Joyce who knew he was drunk?'

'No,' Frankie said painfully. 'She didn't know. Not until Mark told her.' She caught her breath. 'But I hadn't told Mark,' she said. 'And nor had anyone else.'

6

'They're not back yet, I'm afraid,' Mrs Rogers said. 'I had expected them back some time ago, so they shouldn't be long.'

'It's important that I see Miss O'Brien,' Mark said.

'Why don't you come in and wait, Mr Rainford? I can get you a cup of tea, at least. Or you might prefer beer? It's getting very close again.'

'Beer would be very nice,' Mark said.

'You'll be quite comfortable in here,' Mrs Rogers said, opening the door to the sitting-room. 'I'll only be a moment.'

She came in with him and disappeared down the corridor to the kitchen.

Mark looked round the room with its elegant, expensive furnishings and its turn-of-the-century fixtures and fittings. The fireplace with a mantelpiece that you could keep chickens on, the polished doors, the old-fashioned french windows, which had been standing open to the world that night.

He pushed them open now and strolled on to the terrace. The evening sun was warm, but the terrace was in shade, and it made a nice civilised place to sit on a summer evening.

The idea of Frankie disrupting the Edwardian calm of this house appealed to him. He sat down at the wooden table and breathed in the heavy, warm air.

'Oh, there you are! I thought I'd lost you,' Mrs Rogers said. 'It is nice out here, isn't it?' She put down a glass misted by the cold beer. 'I'm sure they won't be long now,' she said. As she turned to go back in, she wheeled round again. 'I almost forgot. Mrs Rainford rang about half an hour ago, looking for you. There's a phone in the hall, if you'd like to ring her.'

Mark smiled and ran his finger up the glass. 'I don't think I will,' he said. 'But thank you.'

'And if Mrs Rainford rings again?' Mrs Rogers asked, though she clearly disapproved.

'Let your conscience be your guide, Mrs Rogers,' Mark said, sipping the beer through the froth. 'I've never found much use for one myself.'

7

'No!' Frankie protested. 'I didn't realise, not then! I thought Mark had seen him and was just keeping quiet about it because he didn't want to get involved. It was David that I thought was lying!' She sat up. 'Mark was at Richard's house. Mrs Milray *saw* him. And how could he have known that the house was deserted all that time if he wasn't there? How could he have known there was a chiming clock?

'And I did think then that it might have been Joyce – but it couldn't have been, because she was in her garden at ten to nine, and it takes too long to get up the hill.' She took Sylvia's hands. 'I didn't know what to think. I still thought it had to have been David.'

'I didn't have an alibi,' Sylvia said with a weak attempt at a smile. 'I was just driving around. Was I on your list?'

'No,' Frankie said. 'Because you thought it was me. And don't you see?' She tightened her grip. 'I was at the quarry about a quarter of an hour after I spoke to Alan. So it all had to happen in fifteen minutes. It had to be someone who was there immediately after he rang me. And you weren't with him, because he was looking for you.' She let go. 'I know where everyone was then, too. Mark was talking to Mrs Milray, just across the road. Joyce was in the garden, David was leaving the quarry and Richard was just on his way there.'

Sylvia didn't mean the doubt that she felt to show in her face, but obviously it had.

'Richard and David didn't meet because they used different paths,' Frankie said, answering Sylvia's unspoken question.

'Then why did Richard say they did?'

'He *didn't*!' Frankie made herself take a breath. 'He said that he'd heard someone. About five hundred yards from the quarry. He'd have reached there at about twenty past nine.' She shivered suddenly. 'The only person he could have heard was Mark.' She swallowed hard. 'It couldn't have been Joyce, because she was too far away. It couldn't have been you or me, because we were together by then.' She was biting her lip in an heroic effort not to cry. 'It couldn't have been David, because by that time he was at the summerhouse, listening to the music from the *Deer Hunter*. And the only way he could have heard that was to be there.'

Sylvia put her hands on her shoulders. 'Frankie,' she said, 'please don't misunderstand this, but isn't it a case of Mark's word or Richard's? You don't *know* which one of them is telling the truth.'

'No,' Frankie picked up her untouched brandy and swirled the fluid round in the glass. 'But I know which one is telling a lie.'

Sylvia sighed. Frankie was coming down from her tightrope at last.

'I couldn't see how Mark could possibly know that Richard's house was deserted,' she said. 'It would have taken him too long if he'd looked for Richard and *then* gone to see Alan. If he'd taken that much time, I'd have seen him at the quarry, because he only had about fifteen minutes all together. But he had seen it, hadn't he? He said it was like the *Marie Céleste*. The lights twinkling on and off and the place as silent as the grave – that's what he said.'

She put down the glass and looked up at Sylvia.

'David thought that the party was still going on, but he only heard the music. From the tape that I put on at half-past six. It ran for three hours, and Richard just left everything as it was when he went. So it carried on playing until half-past nine. And if Mark had been there from nine o'clock, it *wouldn't* have been as silent as the grave. He'd have heard music. The *Deer Hunter* amongst other things.' She paused. 'But as it was, he didn't get there until later. Quarter to ten, I expect, since he heard the clock chime. By that time, it was exactly as he described it.'

Sylvia didn't speak.

'Mark knew all the guests had gone, from Mrs Milray. And he saw Richard in the wood – he had to hide from him. So he knew that Richard must have left his house at about nine, and he thought he was safe in saying what he did.'

Her voice broke on the last word and the tears that she had fought so valiantly couldn't be held back.

Sylvia knelt beside her, holding her in her arms. 'It's all right, baby,' she whispered. 'It's all right.'

It wasn't the first time she had comforted Frankie; she didn't suppose it would be the last. Because Frankie, brave as a lion, would always go where angels feared to tread and find that she didn't much like it when she got there. Sylvia held her close. 'We'll sort it out,' she said. 'Don't worry. We'll sort it out.'

8

Mark drank the beer slowly, enjoying the calm of Hascombe's garden in the evening sunshine. The last time he'd seen it the place had been silent and deserted as though everyone had been spirited away, and he had walked cautiously to the house, thinking that something else must have happened.

Mrs Milray had said that Joyce had gone home with Frankie. His only thought had been to leave the strange, deserted house, and find Joyce. But he'd found Frankie and Sylvia instead, and had had to think on his feet again.

And all because he had changed his mind. He had seen Blake's car, and an unfamiliar emotion had stirred him. It had even taken him a moment to recognise it as anger. Blake had blackmailed Joyce. She hadn't called it that and neither, of course, had Blake. Blake had said that one good turn deserved another, and Joyce had gone along with him, afraid of the consequences if she didn't.

And so he hadn't gone to apologise to Hascombe. Instead, he'd crossed the road to Blake's house. The front of the house was in darkness, and he had walked round the back, pushing open the gate with a squeak. The back door had opened, and Blake had appeared at the gate, drunk and belligerent, thinking it was Sylvia.

And Mark had seized the opportunity that the element of surprise and Blake's inebriation presented to a devout coward like himself. He had punched him. He hadn't even done that right, he reflected. The blow only just made contact, as Blake stumbled back and fell on to the wall, scattering the stones.

He had waited for him to get up, but he had known, really. The whole thing had taken about two minutes, and Blake was dead. Appalled, Mark had pulled him up, trying to make him alive again. But he was dead and the police would want to know why.

Unless . . . it was the quarry stone that had given Mark the idea.

He finished his beer, and waited.

9

Frankie had told Richard, never once looking at him. She stared into her untouched brandy, running her finger noiselessly round the glass. They were alone in Sylvia's drawing-room, and she wanted to go home.

Richard stood up and held out his hand to help her up. She was aware that she had left her raincoat in David's studio and had to tell herself that it didn't matter. Everthing seemed to matter.

'You thought it was me, yesterday,' Richard said. 'At the quarry. You thought it was me, didn't you?'

'Yes,' Frankie admitted guiltily.

'I was following you,' he said. 'You were in such a funny mood. I was worried. When I saw you going up to the edge, I didn't know what I thought.'

She took his hand and got to her feet. 'Let's go,' she said.

The short walk seemed to take forever, because all Frankie wanted was to be inside her own house. Either of them.

They opened the door to the sitting-room and the curtains moved slightly in a current of warmish air; the french windows were open, just like that night when Richard had been so angry with her.

'I'll just see Mrs R about coffee,' Richard said.

She tried to picture Richard at seventy; David had scared her, saying that. But then young men did scare her, with their black and white values and their certainty. Nothing was certain; look at Alan, look at Mark.

She saw Mark's car first; it was parked at the side of the house, its bonnet just visible through the window. So it was no surprise when she saw Mark.

'You've guessed,' he said, standing in the window, a beer glass in his hand. 'Don't ever play poker, Frankie.'

Richard came back as he spoke.

'Thank you,' Mark said, indicating the beer. He looked back at Frankie. 'I've just spent all afternoon with the police,' he said. 'They don't really know what to do with me. They weren't

187

investigating a murder, the inquest didn't say it was murder and I maintain that it was just a pulled punch. They're sorting it out now. I think I'm out on bail, while they write to the DPP or something.'

Frankie sat down, feeling as though her strings had just broken. 'Why, Mark? Why did you take him to the quarry?'

Mark smiled. 'Oh, it wasn't a guess was it? You've worked it all out.' A short sigh escaped him. 'It was an accident,' he said. 'I just thought it ought to *look* like one. I didn't need all the hassle. And I wouldn't have had any if it hadn't been for that ridiculous note. You didn't produce that to protect me,' he said. 'Who did you think you were protecting? Sylvia?'

'No,' Frankie said. 'It was Richard who thought it was Sylvia.' She almost smiled. 'Sylvia thought it was me and I thought –' she shrugged. 'It doesn't matter,' she said. 'But I didn't produce the note. It was an accident too.'

'Anyway, I came to apologise.'

Richard frowned. 'Shouldn't you be apologising to Sylvia?' he said.

'No.' He leant languidly against the french window. 'It seems to me that Frankie was the one who got it in the neck. Sylvia lost a husband that she should never have found and might even collect on the insurance. Joyce got rid of someone who was blackmailing her, whatever he chose to call it. You've got a little business to revive and you're enjoying every minute of it. David got rid of an interloper. It made no difference to me one way or the other, except that I did it, and Frankie got all my flak. I might not have much of a conscience, but I do believe in fair play.'

Frankie listened to his speech and wondered if he really felt as little as he said. 'What's going to happen?' she asked.

Rainford spread his hands. 'It depends on whether or not I'm believed, I suppose,' he said. 'You believe me, don't you?' he asked.

'Yes,' she said.

'Thanks.' He put down the glass and wandered out. A moment later the car drove off.

Frankie closed the windows. 'So that's that,' she said quietly. 'Somebody had better tell Mrs Milray.'

10

Joyce heard the door close and jumped from her seat.

'Where have you been? The police said you'd left hours ago! They want you to ring them.'

Mark took off his jacket. 'Because you've made them think I've skipped the country,' he said.

He looked as though he'd been to report a stolen car. A little irritated, but on the whole optimistic. Nothing was ever important to Mark. Nothing at all.

'I thought you'd left me,' she said.

She couldn't ever remember seeing astonishment on Mark's face before. It made him look younger.

'Me?' he said. 'Leave you? Why on earth would I do that?'

She looked round the room, everything once again where it ought to be. 'I don't let you be very comfortable here, do I?' she said.

'But of course you do!' He sat down. 'Look at it. It's beautiful.' He patted his knee.

Joyce sat down, her arms round his neck. 'But I'm always tidying you up and cleaning everything. You called me a pathological housewife.'

Mark grinned. 'You called me a compulsive gambler,' he said. 'That doesn't mean we don't like each other.'

Joyce smiled. For the first time in her life, she didn't have a game plan. She didn't know what would happen tomorrow. She didn't know what would happen to the house or the fridge-freezer or the three-piece suite. And for the first time in her life, she didn't care.

Mark might go to prison, but if he could handle that, then so could she. It was out of their hands, and worrying wouldn't alter anything.

Besides, it took all the fun out of not being dead yet.

189

Epilogue

Twelve-thirty on a Saturday afternoon in July, and the villages known as the Caswells were receiving yet another downpour.

In Lower Caswell, the gardens were in danger of flooding, as they always were during wet summers. The cobbles of the estate gleamed in the rain, and the JL 4 PR TRUE chalked near the ornamental shrubs was slowly being washed away.

Little boys sheltered under one of the archways, their voices echoing off the damp curved walls, their track-suits spotted with the rain that had stopped play. Somewhere a mother's voice was calling; a child went running off home through the heavy rain. His proud boast was that a man that had done a murder had lived in his house before they did. His mother said that he had got off scot-free; his father said that it had all been a storm in a tea cup and that he had only been charged with manslaughter. But his mother had said that he hadn't gone to prison and that wasn't right.

The pub was full, as usual, but the landlord had lost some custom because of the rain. His chairs and tables in the garden were awash, and the people who had fled had got into their cars and gone home. They didn't like being in the pub now because of the Space Invaders. They said they didn't come to a country pub to listen to bleeps and white noise. But he said he had to move with the times. He had a living to make and the estate residents to consider.

There were no shops in the Caswells; the residents had put up a fight when the general store was sold for building land, but two cottages were almost completed where the shop had been. The rain battered noisily on to the polythene that protected the roof-beams.

Long Caswell never changed much; the houses were even more expensive and there was a corresponding drop in the number of dailies and au pairs. There was, after all, only so much money to go round. The cars were older than they used to be, like the residents.

Inside one of the desirable residences, a man worked at a desk in his study. He was approaching sixty and his short hair was almost all grey. He was pressing keys on a computer keyboard and watching columns of figures displayed on a screen. He rubbed his eyes and swivelled away from the screen to look at a painting on the wall.

It was of a land devastated by war; all around, buildings had been reduced to rubble and the ground cratered by bombs. A huge piece of the landscape had been torn away and the swords and spears of earlier wars revealed. A jet fighter, black as death, swooped in low. In the foreground, petrol bomb in hand, a girl stood waiting for it. She was too thin, she was tired and her hair was dark against her pale skin. But she was ready for the enemy, and she looked out of the picture with eyes of indestructible green.

It was drawn and coloured strip-cartoon style; it wasn't great art. But he would have paid a great deal of money for it. As it was, he was given it by the model.

The road ran out of Long Caswell, past the last and largest of the houses, through Upper Caswell, where the rain streamed down the steep sides of the quarry, which they were talking about filling. There had been a suggestion that refuse might be dumped there, but the CRA was going to fight to the last man on that. There *were* no residents in Upper Caswell to belong to the association, and refuse had to be dumped somewhere, according to the Market Brampton District Council.

The by-pass ran into Market Brampton, where the rain had caught the Saturday shoppers, who sheltered in doorways and went for tea and hamburgers, so the cafés were quite happy about the weather.

The road went past an end-of-terrace house where a telephone rang and was automatically answered. A girl's voice apologised to the caller for her absence; the caller left no message.

Upstairs in the shaded bedroom, a couple were dressing. She was just over thirty, but looked younger. He was almost twenty-two and looked disconcertingly like his mother.

The rain fell past the window on to the young man's car, parked in the side-street below. Across the road, a dark-haired, well-dressed woman loaded shopping into the boot of her car. More than usual, because her son was home before starting work in London, drawing story-boards for TV advertisments. She glanced up at the house as she closed the boot and then at the young man's car and sighed. A man who was passing saw her lips move as she spoke under her breath. He couldn't be sure, but she seemed to say:

'Oh, Frankie.'